9

D1515602

GOODBYE, CHARLI—
THIRD TIME LUCKY

GOODBYE, CHARLI— THIRD TIME LUCKY

•

DIANE PETIT

AVALON BOOKS
THOMAS BOUREGY AND COMPANY, INC.
401 LAFAYETTE STREET
NEW YORK, NEW YORK 10003

PRINTED IN THE UNITED STATES OF AMERICA
ON ACID-FREE PAPER
BY HADDON CRAFTSMEN, BLOOMSBURG, PENNSYLVANIA

To gracious Peggy, who introduced me to "The Cane."

"Stairs, bloody stairs."
—Gertrude Trent

Chapter One

Death remains the greatest equalizer. The handsome, the rich, the young, the old. When their final breath dissipates, leaving their silence the mere echo of life, everyone looks dead. Perpetually cold. Horrifyingly empty. Unnervingly still.

The corpse stared at me. Stared at me from the bottom of a six-foot ice chest. A sheen of frost lent his seemingly unblemished form the eerie impression that he'd merely selected a poor nap location. Someone had taken the time to fold the man's hands together. Rest in peace.

"Gertrude?" I called to the woman waiting several feet away, the woman who was expecting me to expose the preserved body of her beloved dog, Winston. Hopefully the older woman's heart was in better condition than her damaged hip.

"Yes, Kathryn? Is he quite ghastly?" Her voice was molasses-coated gravel.

Gertrude Trent, my latest client, had cautioned me that she hadn't had the heart to check on the bulldog's remains in over five years. Her story was that she was still wrestling with the decision to have the dog's body delivered to a taxidermist. Meanwhile, she'd put the decision on ice, so to speak.

Without touching it, I scanned the corpse for visible marks of violence. Monkey business for sure. People don't stumble into fifty-year-old Sears freezers and lock themselves in. It gave new meaning to the phrase "frozen stiff."

1

Since I'd started my estate sale business, Good Buys, I've "stumbled" upon one mystery after another. But murder? *Another* murder? I couldn't help considering that if this trend didn't stop, people might begin feeling leery of hiring me.

"Gertrude, I think you're going to have to take a look at this," I replied.

"Of course." Gertrude closed the distance between us, tolerating her new awkward gate with determination. Her two hip surgeries had rendered walking painful and challenging. As she was no longer able to manage her huge, rambling three-story, Gertrude had become the first person to hire me to liquidate their *own* estate.

"Great Scott!" Gertrude cried, clutching the side of the freezer, peering intently into the man's face. "It's Mr. Tortelli."

I had been prepared to deal with a shocked, possibly hysterical older woman. Gertrude appeared to be analytically surveying the body. Not for the first time, she had surprised me. There are times, such as this, that I'd give a hand-carved camelback sofa for the ability to do background checks on prospective clients. The daring part of me suspected that practice would take the fun out of exploring (did I say "exposing"?) interesting lives.

"Where on earth is Winston?" Gertrude asked, her voice a combination of hurt and outrage. She recovered quickly.

"Fetch me a flashlight, Kathryn." She motioned briskly behind her. "There should be one in the next room, hanging near the banister."

I did as I was told. How she could know where anything was in this labyrinth of a cellar was beyond me. I'd never seen anything quite so much like the famed catacombs in my life. The basement stretched on and on with room after dark, dank room. Each area proved filled with storage closets and chifforobes that appeared as though they hadn't been touched since the Second World War. The cellar smelled of mold, mildew, and ancient dreams. Now it seemed redolent of death.

"Here you go." I handed Gertrude the flashlight.

She flicked it on. A spot of white light brought the corpse into shocking relief.

"You know this man?" I asked, finding his chalky features vaguely familiar. Thank goodness, no one had shoved him into one of the many hidden cubbies. I've never smelled a ripe corpse and have no desire to do so. My friends in the police department have assured me that there's nothing quite like the stench.

Gertrude sighed, the first hint of emotion to sneak past her resolute manner. "Yes, indeed. This is Mr. Guy Tortelli. He was one of my favorite guests."

My client's passion for taking in strays would have been legendary had she been less circumspect. Once she had allowed a bag woman to reside with her for a full four years. Gertrude simply took the lady home and treated her like a sister until the woman had died. Other people had come and gone as paying boarders or mysterious guests. Now, the place proved populated by the legions of cats that she had adopted and "fixed."

"When was the last time you saw him?" I asked, peering over her shoulder. I'm a tall, big-boned woman. In Gertrude I perceived what future awaited a female such as I. Perhaps the inches I'd lose in height would settle genially around my hips. My figure would grow more imposing and prove capable of providing a fine shelf for children to deposit their weary heads and trials upon.

A sudden non-grandmotherly image of my new client hefting an ax dripping with blood reminded me how deceiving appearances could prove.

"Let's see. It would be five years ago come August. He came and went as he pleased. Would stay for two or three months at a time and disappear. I always wondered why he hadn't returned."

Gertrude tucked her maroon cardigan sweater tighter around her. Frigid air continued blasting noisily from the stalwart freezer. She drew a floral handkerchief from her cleavage and sneezed powerfully into it.

"I suppose we'd best be notifying the authorities," she said, stowing the hanky in a pocket of her pleated charcoal pants.

Before either of us could move, a flurry of orange seemed to descend out of nowhere. The enormous marmalade cat landed square on Mr. Tortelli's chest.

"Nakita!" Gertrude cried.

Having executed a perfect pounce, the cat performed a semicircle, carelessly landing one huge mottled paw in the corpse's face.

"Now you've done it," my employer said, snatching the ponderous feline to her chest. "Tampering with physical evidence." She clucked and stroked the cat, clearly finding its performance more amusing than bothersome. "Won't the coroner be put out with you?"

Turning to me, she said, "Best close him up, Kathryn, before anything else decides to settle on him."

As I eased the freezer door closed, I noticed that Nakita had painted paw prints like frosted roses over the body. Reminded me of *Pilgrim at Tinker Creek,* only without the blood. I couldn't help cringing. Gertrude's careless acceptance of the cat's behavior felt unnerving.

I wasn't intimidated by the coroner. It was the police. This wouldn't be the first time I had found myself playing a bit part in a murder mystery. It's rather inevitable that when I'm settling estates secrets emerge. Is it my fault that some of those secrets prove criminal?

"I'll lock this back up," I said, securing the old padlock and carefully pocketing the heavy key. "Then, I think we'd better talk."

She was already shuffling away. Nakita studied me from

her shoulder. His eyes glinted yellow and malicious. Gertrude waved her free hand in an attitude of dismissal.

"I'll phone the police," I heard her say. "And then I'll call the Home."

She turned and fixed her keen gray gaze on me. "I'll tell them that I won't be checking in just yet. It seems we've got a murder to solve."

"We?"

Nakita leapt free and bounded away into the darkness. Gertrude drew her carved and painted cane from the corner where she'd left it. With the added support, she swung herself around and answered. "Certainly 'we.' Why, it's my house and he was my guest. Don't fret, Kathryn," she said, hauling herself up the first stair. "I won't let you slow me down."

Despite her fierce determination, by the time we'd reached the front parlor and a telephone, Gertrude's complexion had blanched from the effort. Pain pinched her eyes and furrowed her forehead. She collapsed gratefully onto a worn wingback chair. A pair of sprightly Siamese cats leaped clear as she descended.

"Stairs. Stupid stairs." Her chest rose and fell. I had the impression she was either attempting to swallow the pain or expunge it on the out breath.

"Can I get you anything?" I asked.

"You wouldn't have a new hip in that contraption of yours, would you?" Gertrude nodded at my signature black backpack.

Inside it I carried just about everything except prosthetics.

"Sorry," I said, glancing around. It was the sort of room whose haphazard decor fit crazily together in an eclectic mosaic reflecting an owner with a curious life. Who *was* Gertrude Trent anyway?

Five-foot tapestries from Nairobi gazed over Indian cuspidors. The furniture might have been harvested at resale shops like my partner and friend, Jewel's.

Before I could ask her whether she had any painkillers, a familiar scratching called from outside the front door.

"I think your dog is looking for you," Gertrude said. Some color had returned to her face. A knowing smile quirked her thin-lipped mouth. "Why don't you let him in?"

When I'd arrived earlier, Charli, my Brittany, had definitely been more interested in the grounds and its population of cats and squirrels than this job. Gertrude had suggested that we let him run loose since several years back she'd fenced in the estate for just such occasions. Her volunteer work at the Humane Society had taught her the preventive value of a good fence.

"Hand me the phone. I'll call the police, while you get the door."

I passed her a portable phone and headed for the front foyer. The actress in me wanted terribly to answer the door in the persona of a butler. My made-over man's suit seemed a fitting costume. Sweeping my taupe derby off my head and fixing a stiff expression on my face, I prepared to meet my canine companion.

"Good afternoon . . ." I began, as I swung wide the large oak door. Rectitude fled in the face of what I can only describe as a cacophony of pet life tearing past me.

A svelte black cat sped into the parlor with Charli in full pursuit. His stub of a tail flew straight out as he charged around the corner, oblivious of the umbrella stand, which one of them sent crashing to the floor.

I bent to retrieve the assorted umbrellas and canes, which had rolled free like giant pickup sticks. From the next room, I heard Gertrude raising her voice to say, "We have a dead body!" over the sound of ceramic shattering and wood clattering.

Gaining the doorway, I discovered Gertrude yelling with one hand over her ear.

"This is Gertrude Trent. Trent, not Bent!"

The black cat padded soundlessly around the sofa twice with Charli racing behind him. I grabbed the dog by his collar just as the cat sprang to the safety of a marble mantel above the brick fireplace.

The cat began languidly licking its paw as Charli's tongue lolled stupidly from his mouth.

"Charli!" I scolded. He had the decency to look momentarily chagrined.

Gertrude called her address into the phone.

"Enough," I said sternly. He sat obediently and canted his head to fix me with a gaze that read, "What's *your* problem?"

How can anything with such adorable fluffy ears be so much trouble? Charli had always been powerless around squirrels. I'd never noticed him being challenged by cats before. I shoved some of my frizzy blond hair behind my ear. Where was my hat?

"Come here, boy," Gertrude said. She'd hung up the phone and now greeted my recalcitrant dog as though he were an honored guest instead of a canine menace. "What a fine spirit you have. Nice coat."

She stroked Charli's back and the luxuriant snowy fur on his chest. "Do you give him an occasional dose of oil?"

"No," I replied, picking up the pieces of a cheap vase. "He keeps himself groomed."

After surveying the room, I deduced that he'd made more noise than damage. I righted the rocking chair that had been knocked over. My hat lay trampled beside it. I punched the crown back into shape.

"I'm sorry about the mess," I said, putting the derby back on. With my hairpins gone flying, the look was simply not the same. And I'd dressed so carefully, toning down my diverse wardrobe for business. Ah, well.

"Think nothing of it," Gertrude replied, peering at the trash can where I'd deposited the remnants of the vase. She drew a small spiral notebook from the pocket of her cardigan. Smiling agreeably, she jotted a notation. "I'll simply deduct the wholesale value minus depreciation from your commission."

I crossed my hands in my lap and stared at her. She wasn't kidding.

This was going to be a very interesting sale . . . if I survived it.

About ten minutes later, the doorbell rang. Gertrude directed me to answer. I really was feeling quite the butler.

Charli trotted amiably at my heel.

"Quit sucking up," I told him. "You know better than to 'chase game' in the house."

He remained fixed at my side, apparently determined to remind me of his good qualities.

As I swung the door open, the greeting I'd prepared froze on my lips. I'd expected a couple of uniforms to arrive first, with the assigned detective to follow.

Instead I found not one, but two of Landview's finest.

"I told you," the female detective said. Phyllis "Phil" Panozzo gifted me with one of her sardonic expressions.

Her imposing male counterpart rolled his shoulders beneath his leather bomber jacket. He fought a smile and won.

Without taking his formidable gray eyes off me, Detective T. Cole drew a crisp twenty from his fine leather wallet. Phil accepted the offering with elfish delight.

"I was in dispatch when the call came in," Phil said, shoving the bill of her Cubs cap higher on her head. "I told him it was you." That explained their arriving instead of a team of patrol persons.

She stooped over and gave Charli a brisk rub. "I'd recognize Mr. Mayhem's bark anywhere."

Charli nuzzled into her caress. I've noticed that he's more attuned to tone of voice than vocabulary. Phil had made "Mr. Mayhem" sound real dreamy.

"And the best part of our little bet is," Phil said, standing, "he takes the case."

I shot Cole a glance. As usual, his taciturn demeanor gave nothing away. As usual, his very male self instigated treacherous feelings somewhere deep in my belly.

Pulling my lips past my clenched teeth, I attempted a smile.

This situation was a toss-up, actually. I've found myself in the middle of investigations headed by either of them. At the moment, I'd have preferred enduring the dubious relationship I have with Phil, my former high school volleyball rival, than "King Cole," as they'd dubbed the imposing man in Detroit.

Since Cole had returned to our little Chicago south suburb from the big city, he'd developed a tough reputation locally.

Phil stuffed her hands in her Cubs jacket and grinned.

She can be so smug.

Turning her attention to Cole, she gave him a neat punch in the bicep. "Hey, if you need any help, just give me a call."

This time, he lost. A genuine smile transformed his craggy features into something quite marvelous. "Appreciate it."

Phil faltered under his intense gaze, then steeled herself and turned to me. "So long, Bogert. It's really great of you to keep us so busy. We're thinking about naming a room for you down at the station. Me? I voted to dedicate a cell. See you later, babe."

I watched her swing her long legs down the sidewalk toward the street. Charli's stub of a tail twitched his goodbyes. Before Cole could shine his light on me, another car pulled up.

A groan escaped. I locked that smile on my face.

Some men are just made for animal skin. It wasn't hard to imagine Sergeant Randy Burns in caveman garb clutching a club in one of his beefy hands. I could see myself as an impala, the clan's next meal.

"Good afternoon, Sergeant," I called politely. I rubbed the toe of my right oxford against my calf. Shine it up a bit.

Burns continued stalking up the front walk. Apparently, my reputation for veracity had been good enough to demand the superior officer's presence, before confirmation of the body. Either that or he couldn't wait to sink his teeth into me again.

Burns stopped an obligatory two feet from me, just close enough so that he could study my every move and still be intimidating. "Ms. Bogert."

"Who's here?" Gertrude called from in the house. I wondered if it were for the first time. Could she see us through the front window?

"The police have arrived," I yelled back.

"Well, see them in."

I noticed Cole and Burns exchange a look. They said nothing.

Cole took in the spacious room, including the antique rope bed in the corner and Tahitian wood carvings near the bookcase, with feigned nonchalance. I knew him well enough to believe that he wasn't missing a thing.

Burns approached Gertrude with a measure of civility.

She'd remained seated in the wing chair looking regal and vital. I felt an urge to paint her in just that pose. Capture the tired magenta blossoms on the upholstery, the bleached moss-green wall behind the chair, her prominent hooked nose, and the arresting arch of her sable eyebrow. The surprising soft corona of salt-and-pepper hair framing her face. No invalid she.

"Ma'am," Burns said.

"Miss Trent," Gertrude corrected.

"Miss Trent . . ."

"Miss Gertrude Trent," she said with a firm nod.

"Yes." Burns coughed. "You called in a report of a dead body."

"I certainly did." Gertrude tipped her head and scrutinized him from head to toe. I wondered if she'd ever taught seventh grade. She had "the look" down pat. "And who might you be?"

"Sergeant Burns, ma'am. And this is Detective Cole."

Her gaze slid momentarily to the right where Cole was studying a wall hanging.

"I heard a woman. Who might she be?"

Burns cast Cole an annoyed glance. I perched on the curved arm of the horsehair sofa. While I'd been unprepared for such entertainment, I'd no compunctions about enjoying it now that it had arrived.

Cole spoke at last. "That would have been Detective Panozzo, ma'am."

"Well, where is she? Why isn't she here? Don't allow the women to work the homicides? Afraid they'll lose their cookies at the get-go? I'll have you know that women have keen deductive skills and true grit. Where is that Panozzo? I want that Panozzo." She stamped the foot of her cane on the rug for emphasis.

I slid my finger over my mouth. The possibility that Gertrude might prove to be more of a burr in their bonnet than I was positively delicious. Ideally, I wasn't allowing an attachment to the person who'd killed Guy Tortelli. I'd truly regret having to take this woman down.

"Begging your pardon, ma'am," Burns said, his face turning the color of good borscht. "But our detectives are assigned on rotation. Detective Cole here was next up."

Gertrude squinted at them both. She drew that notebook from her pocket again. After fetching the pen she'd nested in the curls of her permanent, she made a notation.

"Is that Burnes, B-U-R-N-E-S?" She didn't glance up.

"Forget the 'e'," Burns replied gruffly.

"Very well." Gertrude finished whatever she was writing and flicked the pen closed. After stowing away her supplies, she drew herself to her feet. It was like watching the abominable snowman come to life. An aging Valkyrie wielding cane and notebook.

I'd a feeling I'd be seeing a lot of that notebook.

The three of us watched her falter and then march rigidly to the doorway.

Apparently she realized we hadn't moved. She turned and gave us all a good stiff glance.

"Well? Are you coming?"

Chapter Two

Secrets and intrigue whispered darkly from the corners. The discovery of Mr. Tortelli's demise had altered the cellar for me. Previously, I'd found it unnerving, possibly fascinating. With the bright sun-splashed hallway at my back, the basement proved sinister and foreboding. Faint rustling seemed to herald more than curious cats.

I brought up the rear as the four of us navigated the open wood stairwell. Charli'd decided to show off by loping ahead of Gertrude. His courage must have failed him at the base of the stairs, as I found him waiting there for me after the others had passed.

"Pretty ghoulish, eh boy?" I muttered, letting my fingers graze reassuringly over his soft head.

The open space, where we stood, I'd found typical of the rest of the cellar. Overhead, thick wood beams held the house like Atlas's shoulders. The cement floor slanted toward the yawning mouth of a rusted drain. Neglected walls wept condensation as their cracked skins flaked to the ground, or dusted the tops of the countless cardboard boxes, which were stacked haphazardly around the perimeter of the room.

"Come on," I told Charli. We reached the old canning room, where the freezer stood, just as the other three became impatient for the key.

"Sorry," I mumbled, stepping forward to open the lock.

Sergeant Burns blocked the way. He held his hand out. I plunked the key on his palm.

The old ice chest was a coffin. I felt as though we were grave robbers, not investigators. What act of desperation had sent Mr. Tortelli to such an early and uncelebrated demise?

The lid of the freezer clanged, striking some ancient conduit. Burns stepped to the side, allowing Cole visual access.

"You know this man?" he asked Gertrude.

"In a manner of speaking," she replied. She'd pursed her lips and seemed lost in thought.

"In what manner of speaking?" Cole asked, drawing out his own version of Gertrude's notebook, a lean leather jobbie.

"He boarded here regularly. Nevertheless, I respected his privacy. He seemed to crave it and he behaved as though he'd earned it."

"And how does one earn privacy?" Cole asked neatly.

"Through service. Through giving up more than one might have liked in order to do a job."

"For instance?"

I felt surprised at Cole's obvious patience with her veiled responses. He'd shown me no such reticence on other occasions.

"A woman might be married to a used car salesman. She might be perfectly content to be wife and mother. The husband, on the other hand, chooses politics. Before you know it, he's governor. Through no fault of her own, the wife has become a public figure. So there you go."

Gertrude lectured him gently. I had the distinct impression she was offering him some sort of intelligence test.

"So Mr. Tortelli was a used car salesman?" Burns asked, pulling his face away from the corpse.

Gertrude winced. What a shame. The dear sergeant failed the test.

"So you think Mr. Tortelli was either famous or famous by association?" Cole asked.

He earned a nod. Gertrude replied, "I would venture to

guess that. He'd had little use for socializing within the community. Yet when we visited he did not strike me as a shy man. He obviously had plenty of money, yet he chose to stay here. My assumption would be that he wanted the privacy.''

Whether Burns was feeling left out or he truly felt the need to call the coroner, I couldn't say. Nevertheless, he announced gruffly that it was time to get the coroner and the evidence techs in.

Burns shut and locked the freezer. Charli led the way again as we moved our little party upstairs. I mulled over Gertrude's observations. Mr. Tortelli *had* looked vaguely familiar. If he had been a public figure of some sort, why had he stayed with Gertrude Trent?

Cole seemed inclined to offer Gertrude an arm as she struggled up the stairs, but he didn't. I found myself admiring his understanding. The woman's disability seemed to wear heavily enough upon her. I sensed people's fussing only made her feel more like an invalid.

''Stairs,'' she muttered again. ''Stupid stairs.''

Must be the mantra she chanted for this particular task.

When at last we gained the front room, Gertrude repeated her collapse into the wingback chair. This time, the Siamese cats weren't quite agile enough. One of them yelped when she nipped its tail.

''Sorry, Mao,'' she said tiredly. ''Me aim is off.''

Mao? I made a mental note to myself to ask about her cats' names.

''Kathryn,'' she said, beckoning me closer. ''Be a dear and fetch me a glass of water from the kitchen. Thank you.''

Charli and I left her with the two officers. Burns was noisily calling the coroner and the evidence techs. Cole appeared to be studying a lithograph of the White House

Green Room, which hung in a gallery of similar pictures by the front window.

The kitchen seemed designed to have fed a large, wealthy household plus staff. The vintage appliances alone would be worth a pretty penny to collectors. I rummaged in an oak cabinet by the sink until I found a glass that didn't appear too dirty.

I decided to wash it anyway.

As I rinsed soap suds off the sides, Charli growled deep in his throat. I glanced down.

His ears were perked. The tail poised straight out. His attention appeared locked on the door or window behind me.

I made a pretense of continuing washing.

"Someone there, boy?" I asked softly.

He took my question as encouragement. Breaking into full bark, he tore across the room.

Swinging around I caught a glimpse of ash-blond hair flick out of sight. I swiftly put the glass down, grabbed a towel, and made for the door as I dried my hands.

Charli, who'd run back across the kitchen, bounded with me. He loves the chase.

I swung open the storm door. The dog dove out, barreling into the legs of a young woman.

She disengaged herself from his now-effusive attentions and gazed up. As she tossed her full shoulder-length hair out of her face, I realized that she wasn't all that young. The promise of wrinkles highlighted her clear complexion. Maturity tinctured her voice. A delicate gold cross glinted from a necklace beneath her chin.

"I didn't mean to surprise you. I noticed the police were here . . . and I was concerned." She met my gaze with a trace of defensiveness. A prominent space between her front teeth merely enhanced an impression of natural beauty.

"Is Gertrude . . . ?" Worry furrowed her brow.

"She's fine," I hastened to say, deciding that this lady was probably only a concerned neighbor.

"Kathryn!" Gertrude bellowed from the other room.

I shared a sheepish grin with the stranger.

"What about that water?" Gertrude called.

"She's in fine voice," I said to the other woman, extending my hand to her. I figured that if Gertrude could make that much noise, her water need wasn't urgent.

"I'm Kathryn Bogert. I own Good Buys. Ms. Trent has hired me to liquidate her estate."

"How do you do?" She met my hand firmly. I registered a strong grip and callused palm. "My name is Connie. Connie Baker. I live next door."

She gestured at another sprawling home on the other side of the chain-link fence. Several vans huddled near a long garage. The logo on their sides proved indecipherable, yet familiar.

"I . . ." Connie gave off whatever she was going to say. Her gaze seemed locked on something or someone over my shoulder.

Pivoting, I discovered Detective Cole watching the two of us intently. Always polite, I smiled and said, "Detective Cole. This is Connie Baker. She lives next door. She noticed your cars and came to check on Ms. Trent. Ms. Baker, this is Detective Cole."

Connie tilted her chin higher. Her hand rose unconsciously to that little gold cross. I watched her swallow hard. Poor lady. Maybe she had a fear of authority figures or she'd learned to steer clear of overly handsome men. Either way, I couldn't help wondering how Cole was interpreting her defensive body language.

"Ms. Baker?" he said at last. He wrote the name down.

She nodded. Her blue eyes grew wide and then slanted cautiously.

"And you live next door?"

"Yes."

A tinge of hostility?

He wrote that down, too. He made a show of staring at her house before subjecting her to his firm gaze. Then he walked closer, indicated that I should step back in, and he drew the storm door nearly closed behind us.

"Ms. Trent is fine. Thank you for coming by." He finished closing the door in her face.

I shoved my hands in my pants pockets and struck a pose.

"You're a piece of work, Cole," I said, shaking my head.

Turning my back on him, I retrieved the glass and filled it with tap water.

"She was just trying to be a good neighbor," I pointed out. "Everybody a suspect, eh, Cole?"

He followed me as I walked down the hall.

"That's the name of the game, isn't it, Kathryn?"

Nudging past me, to enter the sitting room first, he caught my eye.

"Especially when the game is murder," he finished.

I kept Gertrude company as the coroner and the evidence techs traipsed back and forth. Charli lay on the floor pawing a rubber mouse. Mao eyed him curiously.

A definite twinkle seemed to have alighted in Gertrude's eye. By the time Burns and Cole returned their attention to us, her color proved excellent and her tongue neatly honed.

"Okay, Ms. Trent," Burns said, hitching up his pants. "We'd like the two of you to come down to the station to answer a few questions."

Cole popped a coffee stirrer into his mouth. I reminded myself to ask him whether he'd ever get over the nicotine demon. I began standing.

"There's no need for that," Gertrude replied, nodding for me to remain seated. She sipped her water. "I'd prefer to talk here."

I tucked my cheek between my teeth to keep a straight face. Cops like to get you down to the station where they can isolate, intimidate, and interview you. It was the drill.

"We won't keep you long," Cole said, shifting the stirrer to the opposite side of his mouth.

"Poppycock," Gertrude said. She held the glass in both hands on her lap. "Any questions you have may be asked right here."

She reached over to an end table and placed the glass on a coaster formed out of a slice of agate.

Across the room, Cole and Burns exchanged a few strongly whispered words. When they finished their confab and separated, Burns appeared barely mollified. Cole proved the designated speaker.

"If you'd be more comfortable here, that's fine. Sergeant Burns will take Ms. Bogert into the kitchen so that we won't be disturbed."

I sighed. Good cop, bad cop. I'd been down this road before. Before I could stand, Gertrude sputtered, "Do sit, Kathryn. You're making me dizzy."

She adjusted her cardigan around herself with a huff. "Any and all questions we may or may not choose to answer can be directed to us right here, right now. I've no use for mind games or police tactics. I intend to give you my full cooperation, but I'll not be inconvenienced to do it."

Did she wink at me?

"At my age, I value my time. Don't waste it."

Burns looked ready to blow. I wondered what his blood pressure was.

Charli leapt onto the couch and sat beside me. Before I could scold him, Gertrude sketched a dismissal. "Let him be. He's just getting ready to answer a few questions, aren't you, Charli?"

The dog looked willing enough.

Cole cleared his throat. As he drew up a straight-backed

cane chair, Burns leaned against a wall. Somehow he'd discovered a bare spot between an aborigine spear and what looked like a Warhol painting of a jar of Postum. He folded his burly arms across his chest and glowered at us.

"When was the last time you saw Mr. Tortelli alive?" Cole asked.

Mentally I congratulated myself for asking the same opening question as the professionals had. I stroked Charli's back while I watched Cole interview Gertrude.

I'd never seen her happier.

She repeated what she'd already told me, adding that her acquaintance with Guy Tortelli had lasted for about eight years. He'd arrived toting a few bags in the early eighties in response to an advertisement that Gertrude had posted in the newspaper.

"Didn't you require references?" the detective asked. His tone of voice conveyed disapproval.

"I never use them. If I'd a problem with someone, it was easy enough to check them out then."

"And Mr. Tortelli was never a problem?"

Gertrude studied the floor. A soft smile accompanied her reply. "No. Guy was never a problem."

She drew her hanky from her pocket and blew her nose. Reaching for her cane, she stood uneasily. I rose as well.

Perhaps I'd imagined her moment of grief. She fixed all of us with an eagle eye and smirked.

"Don't you want to look at his things?"

Chapter Three

"His things?" I said, before the police could reply. "What things would you still have after five years?"

I entertained twisted images of her keeping his room sacrosanct. A shrine to a peculiar affection?

"Why don't you show us to his room?" Cole suggested. The way his teeth were clenched, I wasn't sure what would give out first: a molar or that bit of plastic.

"Oh, you won't find anything *there*," Gertrude said, shaking her head. She paused, pursing her lips. "I suppose it *is* possible, depending on how sophisticated your forensics department is. Well, I'll take you there first."

Charli and I began following Gertrude and the two police officers. At the foot of a Scarlett O'Hara stairwell, Burns turned to face me down.

"You are not needed here," he said. From his position on the bottom step he could look me in the eye.

I glanced up at Gertrude, who had halted her ascent. She rolled her eyes skyward. "Not to worry, Kathryn. Let the men have their little victories."

Charli and I waited at the base of the stairs for them to continue on their way. Gertrude was regaling the officers with stirring tales of the advantages of matriarchal societies in both primitive and ancient cultures.

"Let's get some air," I told the dog.

Truthfully, I felt grateful to be out from under the microscopic scrutiny of our men in blue. I planned to enjoy the reprieve.

We stepped out the front door just as the sun slipped behind a bank of bluish cloud. A chill breeze swept through various mature trees on the expansive lawn. On close inspection, I could see they varied in both leaf and bark. Each appeared to represent a different species. Tumbled around a mound of purple and white crocuses lay a hodgepodge of rocks the size of children's football helmets.

The sturdy chain-link fence seemed quite at odds with the grounds. Rather like putting braces on the Victorian gardens. I wondered at Gertrude's choice. Away from her indomitable presence, I began to wonder quite a few things.

How much did I really know about Gertrude Trent? My work had schooled me in the depths of people's character. Despite what public image he or she might have, each person harbors many lives, some lived, others only dreamed about. What experience had led Gertrude to be so comfortable with death, so confident in her detecting abilities?

As Charli and I strolled toward the street, a half a dozen cats skittered away. The cats proved an assortment a sizes and colors. There seemed to be nothing about Gertrude or her estate mass-produced; everything appeared distinctive.

A one-eyed kitten leered at me from behind a rhododendron.

Charli bounded over to play. The cat rewarded his overtures with a yowl and a swipe of its scrawny paw.

Gertrude was quite a character. Her wit and fortitude did not exclude her as a suspect. On the contrary, if she had killed Guy Tortelli, it would be to her advantage to orchestrate a discovery of the body since it would surely be uncovered when the property was disposed of. What better way to throw the police off guard than to act the detective?

"Do I look jaded, Charli?" I asked the dog. "I think I've been hanging around cops too long. It's rubbing off. Watch yourself, or I'll be asking you where you were and what you were doing five years ago."

The dog studied me with typical good grace. One of the

great things about Charli is that he does a perfect impression of a good listener. I've often wondered what really goes on behind those knowing brown eyes in that canine skull.

Deciding to take my mind off the murder, I thought ahead to the sale, which I felt sure would proceed eventually. It was time to purchase some of those resource books that I'd been borrowing. Without expert assistance there was no way I'd be able to accurately price Gertrude's estate. There was just too much good stuff.

Where did she get all that good stuff? I asked myself, stepping automatically around an old stump. This murder was obviously going to dominate my attention. I wouldn't be alone.

My father, Hyman "Harry" Bogert, loved nothing better than to kibitz my investigations. I could almost see him in my mind's eye, rubbing his hands together. *"Murder again, Katie. What luck!"*

Jewel Johnson, Dad's almost-fiancée and my unofficial business partner, would not be thrilled. *"The last case nearly landed you in the slammer,"* I could imagine her saying. At least Jewel would share my enthusiasm for the sale. It had been she who had gotten me involved in "garage sailing" when I'd been in need of a ready supply of frames during my artist years. We'd authored *The Garage Sale Handbook* together, and the rest was history.

As my mind filled with grand plans for the future, I almost didn't hear the ruckus ahead. Charli barked once.

The sound of stone striking metal, and the unmistakable shrill of a childish taunt, sent me striding through a curtain of winking yellow forsythia.

"Nah, nah. Nah, nah. Bessie Boogie's lost her claw."

A rock whisked past my ear. I didn't appreciate it.

I reached the fence before another projectile went flying. "Hey!" I yelled. "Stop that."

An elderly woman appeared cornered against the chain

link by two scamps, who could have been anyone's little boys. They appeared young enough to have blessedly poor aim, and old enough to have been taught better behavior.

Seeing me, they fled.

"Are you all right?" I asked the woman, who was leaning over retrieving what I assume had tumbled out of her worn canvas tote.

Dusky mushrooms, nuts, crimson berries, and other common yard growth disappeared into the shoulder bag.

She didn't answer me, merely went about picking up her scattered goods. I studied the four-foot fence, making a quick decision.

It only took me a moment to climb to the other side. Charli paced his frustration from the yard.

"Here," I said, handing her what looked like a green walnut.

She hesitated. Looking at me askance, she reached for the nut with her thin, wizened hand.

"Obliged," I think she muttered.

"My name is Kathryn," I said kindly. "Kathryn Bogert."

The way she gazed off down the road made me wonder when she'd last encountered plain friendliness. What a marvelous portrait *she'd* make. The face of a dried apple. Eyes a smoky blue, the color of winter sky pregnant with snow. Pure white hair shot with a single mad streak of black.

She began moving away. Her walking stick, a cast-off oak branch, was no doubt harvested like the rest of her things. It was difficult to tell whether she was as petite as she appeared. Osteoporosis had hunched her over.

On impulse, I fell into step beside her. Charli trotted inside the fence along a parallel path.

"What's your name?" I asked.

No reply. She continued shuffling along in chunky black shoes, bleached white anklets, and the sort of housedress that Jewel wore when she canned tomatoes. It was easy to see why neighborhood kids might make a target of her.

We reached the end of Gertrude's property. Charli pressed his snout through the corner of the fence and snarfed his frustration. I contemplated the officers waiting for me in the house and figured I'd ditched school long enough.

"It was nice to meet you . . ." I said, leaving the end of the sentence hanging in the air like an invitation.

Her voice sounded as though it hadn't been used in a while. I barely heard her response.

"Bessie," she said.

"It was nice to meet you, Bessie," I replied. The neighborhood felt quiet as I watched her walk on. There was a dignity about her, as though she'd asked for and received the earth's permission for every earnest footstep.

I wondered where she was headed. Gertrude's home was one of about eighteen tucked on four blocks, which dipped down toward the river. A neighborhood. Struggling families, tentative couples and now . . . secret death exposed. The two plots on the riverbank were frank about their years. The one on the left hid its neglect behind the gracious fronds of immense willows. To its right a second two-story steadied itself on a slanted porch. Its peeling paint was gray on gray. The only splash of color proved a FOR SALE sign— green and yellow, a local realtor.

Bessie disappeared among the willows.

A peculiar sensation creeps across the back of my neck when someone is watching me. I'd noticed it the first time in second grade when Mrs. Apple caught me talking during a spelling test. First the fingers of apprehension at my nape, then . . .

Peering sideways, I pivoted slowly, casting my glance over the other five homes on the street. The bungalow beside the sale home featured an interesting color scheme: redwood and cream, with navy accents. The political plac-

ards, which dotted the windows and littered the lawn, op-
pressively hawked *Jerry Ritter for Congress. A vote for
Jerry is a vote for decent government.*

In the Cape Cod directly across the street, the curtains
on the living room window fluttered closed. I stared, but
whoever had been spying on me didn't repeat their
performance.

Neighborhoods remind me of onions. Layer upon layer
of relationships, the deeper, tear-urging layers hidden and
fundamental. Who among these people had shared a casual
greeting with Guy Tortelli? Had anyone shared more?

Almost in answer to my question, a red Le Baron swept
into the mouth of Willow Lane. Its driver slowed to ease
past the police cars and then sped carelessly past me into
the Bakers' driveway.

When the blond driver swung out of the car, I wondered
where Connie had tripped off to. Then, Connie Baker and
a beanpole of a man stepped out of the front door of the
rambling ranch house next to Gertrude's.

I did a double take. By the time Connie had enfolded
''Connie'' in an effusive hug, I realized that I wasn't de-
lirious. The woman who had just arrived looked enough
like Connie Baker to be her twin. A closer look revealed
that the driver sported a flashier, shorter hairstyle than
Connie. The man beside them appeared even older than I
had first thought. His etched wrinkles stood in stark contrast
to their vibrant complexions. A strawberry birthmark
spread like spilled brown ink over the right side of his face.

While he stood back from the hugs and expressions of
joy, I sensed a proprietary contentment in his stance, which
seemed at odds with his sinister countenance. When he
caught my eye, a shuttered caution altered his. Surely his
mottled, sullen complexion attracted abuse from the neighborhood children, the sort Bessie endured.

It seemed the activity at Gertrude's and my presence

commanded the Bakers' attention in a way that surpassed simple curiosity. I felt their interest as an unwelcome gaze.

Since they'd already noticed me, there was no way to slip closer and ferret out their conversation. There proved little opportunity to do so. The man shepherded the women into the house without touching them. The younger "Connie" cast a curious glance over her shoulder in my direction, but she complied. By the time their neat blue door closed securely behind them, I'd stepped into the relative obscurity of a rambling evergreen.

Charli had struggled beneath the lowest branches to press his nose against my leg through the fence. The pungent aroma of evergreen enveloped me, clearing my head and making me feel sequestered despite an increasing level of anxiety.

"Secrets. Funny little itching secrets," I said. Peering around the stiff fingers of the cedar I noticed someone else had taken an interest in the arrival of the Le Baron.

Across the street a short man wearing work overalls peered at the Baker home. His black-rimmed glasses concealed his attitude. He had good cheekbones, square shoulders, and a crop of thick sable hair. His mournful expression reminded me a little of Buddy Holly. When he gave off looking at the Bakers', he walked back up the driveway with the cautious gait of a person treading through a light rain, their eye on the sidewalk instead of the path ahead.

I had little time to contemplate the stranger's interest in the Bakers.

Suddenly, a distinctive roar sounded at the corner house by the cross street. Louder than a teen's stereo, more relentless than a snowblower, able to shake loose dentures with a single pass . . .

A trio of Big Wheels clamored closer and reeled into the Bakers' driveway with the reckless bravado of a motorcycle gang. The point man, who I recognized as one of the rock throwers, navigated a clumsy black "tricycle" with a dented front wheel. Behind him, a tow-haired boy spun perilously close to the fender of the Le Baron before wheeling out of the drive behind the first boy.

The final wheeler pedaled vigorously in their wake. I registered a crop of auburn curls and a stained gray sweat suit.

Before I could scream, "Get a license!" the moppet eased to a stop before me, demonstrating a certain grace and peculiar radar.

I found myself peering into the cherubic face of a one-eyed, pint-sized child, female variety. One of those cloth patches blended across her right eye. Having "parked" at my feet, her hands moved into "ready position." The left one twirled a curl and the right thumb plunked contentedly into her mouth.

"Whatcha doin'?" she asked, around her thumb. She peered up at me as though she were accustomed to finding women lurking in bushes and had never been taught to be leery of strangers.

"Hiding," I replied, honestly.

She nodded, her unruly ringlets bobbing merrily. Foregoing asking permission, she scrambled off her Big Wheel, without disturbing the thumb, and stepped into the shade beside me.

I smothered a grin as I looked down at her head, which barely reached my thigh. She was staring out as though she were analyzing my choice of hideaway.

Charli offered a muffled greeting and nudged her side.

"Doggie!" she cried. The thumb popped free as she reached both hands through the chain link to capture Charli's ears and yank them toward her.

Before I could utter a word of caution, she'd begun nuzzling his snout in a way that was positively revolting. Surely she had no clue all the interesting places that snout had been. Thank goodness Charli loved kids.

"What's your name?" I asked, easing my dog's ears free. Charli liked children, but he was also attached to his ears. Her mighty fists had threatened to scalp him.

" 'Manda," she replied, again around the thumb.

"Amanda?"

She blinked and nodded. I was guessing her age to be an inarticulate, but highly mobile twenty-four months.

" 'Manda!" I heard a boy scream. Apparently her sibs had finally noticed that the caboose had derailed.

" 'Manda go now," she said solemnly, climbing back on her Big Wheel. With a look of pixie determination she clattered to the end of the driveway. If I didn't know better, I'd swear she was trying to avoid revealing my hiding place to the others.

"I think we'd better get back into the house," I told Charli. I stepped away from the cedar. We repeated our earlier trail until I reached the spot where I'd rather ignominiously hopped the fence. "Might as well take the long way around," I said.

Charli stayed with me, dodging small shrubs and several trees. When I reached the driveway, I found it burgeoning with vehicles. Quite festive looking, except the absence of people. I picked my way past the coroner's car as I headed for the front door. Whether they were finished looking at Mr. Tortelli's room or not, I intended to do a little exploring in that basement. Gertrude had mentioned something about storage for her guests and I wanted to check it.

With luck, I'd manage a peek before the officers kicked me out.

Chapter Four

I made it past the main floor without being detained. It wasn't until we'd reached the basement that I was apprehended.

"Ms. Bogert," Cole called at my back. Busted.

I froze, a vital step away from the yawning privacy of a darkened corridor. Turning slowly, I erased guilt from my features.

"Going somewhere?" he asked. He had a way of making his voice smile despite a deadpan expression.

"I think I left my backpack down here," I answered cheerfully.

"Your backpack is in the front parlor," he replied.

The coroner slipped out of the canning room and lumbered up the stairs. He was a man who could charitably be called copious.

"Is it? I'd better go check. I have a feeling I need to powder my nose." I stepped stoutly toward the stairs intending to retrace the coroner's path. Strong, masculine fingers found the flesh at my forearm.

"There's nothing the matter with your nose, except its proximity to this case," Cole said.

Why did his deep voice and firm touch do such disturbing things to my equilibrium? Perhaps I'd been without a relationship for too long. My ex, Gary, had frankly soured me on love. Grand passion and self-dissolving romance were overrated in my opinion. I'd been committed to myself for some time and to a solitary pursuit of life, me, and an occasional mystery.

I glanced down at his hand. He seemed to take notice of his gesture. Whether he found it inappropriate, I couldn't say. He did linger a moment before relinquishing his hold.

"Did you find anything of interest in Mr. Tortelli's room?" I asked, hoping to deflect the tension in the air and possibly garner some facts.

He smiled, earnest, full, and devastating. Here was the archetype for the romantic detective. Too rugged to be pretty. Too compelling to be plain. He smelled of lush woods and tangy dew-kissed dawns.

"You're going to interlope on my investigation, aren't you?" he said.

"Your investigation is interloping on my sale. It's a question of perspective. Besides," I said, letting my fingers flutter like butterflies of possibility, "someone has to keep Gertrude in line."

"Someone meaning you? That's a bit like asking Beavis to monitor Butt-head."

"Really, Detective. If I were the sensitive type I'd be positively insulted."

Cole lapsed into cryptic silence, studying me with that unnerving gaze. Then his attention shifted to the corridor behind me, as though he'd only now taken notice of my trajectory.

Before he could query me further, the unmistakable sound of Gertrude making her descent carried into the room.

". . . stairs."

I heard Burns mutter something and then Gertrude protesting, "No, I don't need a hand, Sergeant. Don't be trying any fussy fingers with me."

They joined us a minute later, Gertrude flushed with power, Burns beet red with something less heady.

"Kathryn," Gertrude cried, "there you are. We were just

about to check out Mr. Tortelli's storage locker. Good of you to join us.''

She arched an eyebrow at me in a way that implied she'd deduced my premature venture and heartily approved of it.

"Okay, where is it?" Burns asked gruffly. He peered around at the four major corridors, which fed out of this close space like the pulsing blood vessels of a heart.

"Let me see now," Gertrude drew out, pursing her lips, and tipping her eyes up and to the right as though she were trying to remember.

Burns sort of groaned.

Smothering a smile, Gertrude said at last, "I believe it's this way." She pointed with her cane to the entryway where Cole had intercepted me. Inwardly, I congratulated myself again on my instincts.

As the four of us, with Charli gamely in the rear, made our way down a hall, which bore no small resemblance to an old prison, those instincts addressed me again.

Answers lay hidden in one of these iron-gated storage cells. I could feel it in my bones.

"Would somebody get Rin Tin Tin out of my way!" Burns said with annoyance.

Charli had slipped ahead, grazing the sergeant's leg. Purposefully, he'd plopped himself in the burly man's path. His dog body effectively blocked the corridor as he stared into one of the padlocked storage areas.

"Go on," Burns said. "Get."

"Sergeant," Gertrude interjected. "The dog has demonstrated a perception you'd be wise to emulate. There is no need to 'go on,' as you say. We have arrived at our destination. This"—she waved her cane at an area about the size of a decent shed—"is Mr. Tortelli's storage facility."

I peered past Cole's broad shoulders. As I'd already noted, the blackened diamond security gates lining both sides of the corridor gave the appearance of a mini storefront in a rough neighborhood or an old prison. I stared at Tortelli's stash. Looped through the gate's fastening, a combination lock gleamed mockingly from beneath layers of dust.

"Why didn't you ever remove his things?" Cole asked, trying as I was to decipher the contents of the area in the dim light cast by a single filthy overhead bulb. "When he didn't return, why didn't you clean it out?"

"Didn't need the space," Gertrude replied, suddenly somber. "Besides, it would've seemed so final, so irreparable. I'd never gotten a chance to say goodbye to him after all, not goodbye for good."

My heart went out to her. Goodbye for good. Perhaps it's the storyteller in each of us that craves a nice neat ending, an opportunity for closure, a simple, sincere *adieu.*

"You got a bolt cutter?" Burns grumbled, palming the capable lock in his hand.

"In my car," Cole replied.

"Don't you need a warrant or something?" I asked. I don't read mysteries the way my father does, so I'm not hep to all the nuances of police procedure.

"Kathryn, dear," Gertrude said. "It's my house and I've granted my permission. At any rate, Mr. Tortelli is indubitably deceased and certainly not in a position to grant his."

"I'll get the bolt cutter." Cole disappeared down the hallway, leaving us with the good sergeant.

"What's with this setup, anyhow?" Burns drew out a Maglite, shining its solid beam into the cell. Swinging it sideways, he let the white light arch over a dozen similar storage areas.

"My grandmother had the compartments built for tenants. When I chose to occasionally take boarders in, I made use of them, too."

Burns's light tarried on a cell two compartments down that appeared to contain a saddle, boots, and chaps. He

made a harrumphing sound. The sergeant made more trans-
verbal noise than my dog.

I wished he'd focus his light back on Tortelli's space.
Curiosity was proving an annoying partner. I'd spied something that I thought was important behind a cardboard container on an old sideboard.

It seemed to take way too long for Cole to return.

"Sorry," Cole said a few minutes later. "My father must
have taken the cutters out of the trunk. One of the other
officers had a pair, though."

Cole's father, retired police sergeant T. J. Cole, had ter-
rified me for years. He'd been a regular at my father's
barbershop since I was a little girl. Initially, I'd put down
Cole's ability to unnerve me to some familial knack. Now
I wasn't so sure.

"Hand it over."

Cole passed Burns the cutter. The sergeant popped the
lock in a second.

Before his superior officer could take further action, Cole
asked nonchalantly, "Do you want the techs to sweep
through here?"

Burns wore the expression of a restrained bulldog. He
waved one of his hands. "Yeah, get 'em in here. Might as
well keep everything tidy."

I finally shared something genuine with the guy. I had
no use for waiting further either. That glint of metal behind
the box called to me like a siren.

"Hey! You can't—" Burns made an aborted attempt to
prevent Charli from darting into the now-accessible cell.

"Charli!" I cried. No use.

His Brittany body disappeared behind the sideboard. I
heard his nails desperately clawing the concrete near the
back wall.

Before any of us could react, a feline yowl, one short
bark, and the chase was on. It proved blessedly brief, but

unfortunately messy. A cardboard box toppled over. An avalanche of paper flowed beneath four pairs of scurrying paws. Charli crashed into a leg of the sideboard. Scrambling for a foothold, he flung the paper in all directions like a tire entrenched in mud.

The same black cat who had eluded Charli earlier eased through one of the spaces in the grate, leaving the dog caged behind him. Charli appeared momentarily stymied. I could feel my innards curdling. This was just the sort of thing that enhanced my already murky rep with the local cops.

"Anwar," Gertrude said, as the cat curled itself diabolically around her leg. "You are always in the thick of things, aren't you?"

The cat peered up at her, its jet eyes glinting with self-satisfaction.

Charli must have remembered the way in as he trotted back to it. Just as he was about to continue his pursuit of the cat, Cole commanded, "Down."

The dog hit the down position as though he'd been felled by a bullet. I wish he'd listen to me like that.

"I'm going to shoot that darn dog. I swear." Burns appeared angry enough to make real his threat.

"Nonsense," Gertrude said. "You'd have a dozen forms to fill out for discharging your weapon."

I stared at her. What made this seemingly innocuous woman so knowledgeable about such things? *Ah, Gertrude Trent. Are you too clever by far?*

"Kathryn," Cole said, surprising me by dropping my surname. "The dog."

"I'll put him outside," I replied, grasping Charli's choke collar.

As I heeled him away, I wanted to ask them to wait for me, to not go in just yet. Thanks to Charli, I warranted no such consideration. As I made my way up the stairs, I trembled with frustration.

Whatever was behind that box was not going to be discovered in my presence.

"Nice job, Charli," I told him. "If I were you I'd stay clear of Sergeant Burns for the remainder of this case."

He hung his tail and ears in an attitude of total contrition. I wasn't fooled. In some ways, he was like a child. He didn't like being caught. He hated being scolded. But in regards to the original offense? No remorse. None.

I cast Charli outside rather unceremoniously and hustled back toward the basement. This house was definitely not handicap accessible. Tight corners, slim corridors, overstuffed living areas, and steep stairs had me panting by the time I'd returned to the others.

The evidence techs were still checking the area when I arrived. They were snapping dozens of photos and I could feel the tension in the corridor as we waited our turn.

"Lots of paper," a tech said, smacking her gum noisily. "*Lots* of paper."

I wanted to scream, "What's behind that box?" But that would have been childish.

It didn't take long for them to finish. I'm sure that space alone had prevented Burns from going in there with them. When they'd finally departed, he sauntered in, sneering at the mess on the floor.

Cole strode behind him. He must have seen what I'd seen, because his direction proved unerring.

"Typewriter," Cole said, making a note of it. "Manual. Smith Corona."

I stooped and picked up a paper with Charli's paw prints on it. Checking the upper right-hand corner, I held my breath. Above a page of text, was the header *Kordell—Sparkle—page 231.*

Scanning the prose, I read:

. . . Sophia's Bentley hugged the coastline, as she navigated the curves of the Corniche du Littoral, dem-

onstrating a recklessness that only the very rich possess. Death wouldn't dare claim her. Daddy would sue.

Gertrude interrupted me. "What's that? What have you got there?"

Her voice revealed her frustration at not being able to snag a paper herself.

I passed her the sheet in my hand.

Soon, we were all reading. Some pages I'd grabbed had little notes in the margins scrawled in a flourished hand. *Stupid name. Check spelling. What a cad!*

Tucking the papers under my arm, I skirted the sideboard and made for the typewriter. While Cole opened assorted boxes, I let my fingertips slip to the keys of the machine.

Check spelling. Sparkle. Sophia's . . . The words on the page filtered through my mind like a forgotten melody. My fingertips felt warm as though the memory of urgent effort and creative flair had been pressed indelibly into the keys.

Closing my eyes, I imagined Guy Tortelli hunched over this typewriter, pounding out tales, eking out stories, clamoring for inspiration. I felt his presence in this room. His living presence, stowing away first drafts, second drafts, final drafts. A secret cache of dreams.

"It appears you were correct, Ms. Trent," I heard Cole say.

I opened my eyes. Across from me I saw Gertrude's eyes shining with unshed tears.

"Poor Mr. Tortelli," Gertrude said, clutching one of the half a dozen black composition notebooks that we'd found.

"Poor Mr. Kordell," I corrected.

Sergeant Burns shone his light directly on the page in his hand. The potent beam flowed through the paper like a spotlight.

"Who is . . ." Burns squinted. ". . . Cameron Kordell?"

Chapter Five

None of us answered immediately. Personally, I searched for a reply that wouldn't communicate my shock that Burns might be illiterate. Did I mention that I'm still working on curbing my snob instincts?

"Cameron Kordell was a best-selling novelist," Cole replied.

I waited for Burns to ask what Kordell's papers were doing in Tortelli's storage area. Apparently, the sergeant wasn't that obtuse.

"You recognize this handwriting, ma'am?" Burns pointed to a scrawled citation on a manuscript page.

Gertrude blinked twice. "It's Guy's handwriting. He had such a bold hand."

"So . . ." Burns said, lounging against the sideboard and surveying all the boxes of manuscripts and matching piles of black composition notebooks. "It looks like Guy Tortelli edited this Cameron Kordell's books, huh?"

"They're all here," Cole said, searching the labels, which I could now see had been written in black permanent marker. *"Glitter, Sparkle, Neon, Fortune . . ."*

"Hey, I saw *Fortune*," Burns said, enthusiasm lightening his voice. "Farrah Fawcett starred in that one, didn't she?"

"Yes, Sergeant," Gertrude said tiredly. "All of Kordell's books made the rather lucrative transition to television miniseries at one time or another."

She shared a steady glance at Cole and myself. Cole

chose to speak. "Sergeant Burns, it's certainly possible that Guy Tortelli did more than edit Kordell's work. From everything that Ms. Trent has told us, isn't it possible that Tortelli *was* Kordell? That he wrote under that pseudonym?"

Burns wasn't the only one with fond memories of Farrah. My father, who wouldn't have read a Kordell novel if it were the last thing in the library, also entertained a soft spot for the former Charlie's Angel.

"You remember *Fortune,* Jewel?" Dad said, his fork poised over our evening's dessert. It wasn't warm enough to dine in the yard, so we were completing our nightly ritual in the comfort of our spacious Sears kitchen. Not the appliances. The house.

Early in the century our house had been ordered through a Sears catalogue—every board, nail, and window. I used to think that "Sears" was a magical name—it was on everything!

Jewel seemed a bit distracted. She took her time replying. Our friend had one blue eye and one brown. The brown one never quite focused on you and I was forever trying to snag its attention. She tugged at the knot on a long paisley scarf, which she'd worn over her hair.

"I remember," she replied. "Your father was positively drooling during that bathtub scene," she added to me.

"I was not!"

"You were." Jewel smiled generously.

The corner of Dad's mouth quirked. "It's coming back to me." He put his fork down and placed his hand over Jewel's. "But don't worry. Farrah doesn't compare to you."

Jewel blushed furiously. "Oh, get on with you."

If any couple their age could be called "adorable" it would be Jewel and Dad. They'd been special friends for fifteen years, nearly as long as my mother had been dead. Dad was as slow to commit as I. At this point, I felt sure he'd decided to marry Jewel. He was simply taking his time. He was being Dad.

The familiar clunk of heavy plastic striking vinyl floor resonated through our kitchen. We ignored it.

"Gertrude . . ." I began, never to finish my explanation.

Another clunk. We glanced across the room. Dog dish bites the dust.

Charli had a habit of picking up his dish and plunking it noisily down when he wanted to be fed. At the moment, he was no doubt coveting our lemon meringue.

"Dream on," I told him. The dog cocked his head, perking his ears to their fluffiest advantage. "You're lucky they didn't arrest you. Butch, the animal control officer, probably kept a rap sheet on you."

Charli padded across the room and lay his head in my lap, mournful, liquid brown eyes, freckled snout, and all. He had a rust hourglass marking on his face that made his spots resemble sand or tears.

"How can you be angry with him?" Dad said, tossing him a bit of crust. Ever since we'd scrapped his doggy diet, my father had been feeding him from the table. A flagrant violation of our "co-parenting" agreement.

Charli gobbled up the minuscule treat, pathetically grateful.

"That dog ran a marathon through our biggest clues!" I said.

"Brittanies are fine hunting dogs," Dad countered, running his hand over the sparse black hairs slicked over his scalp. His calm maneuver reeked of superiority.

I recalled Charli's checkered hunting history and pinned Dad with a fierce glance.

"Don't even go there," I told him. I decided to change the subject. In our family, we enjoy conversational pinball, letting the ball carom off into the strangest directions. I turned to Jewel.

"What's with the scarf?" I asked. She'd made a point

of wearing it in the house and didn't seem to realize that her fidgeting with it only drew our attention more.

"This old thing?"

It was not an old thing. Well, it was old but not in that manner. It was a vintage piece from her shop, Jewels. The way both her eyes eluded me and her pudgy hands folded and refolded her napkin made me suspicious.

Guy Tortelli's fate was already sealed. The investigation could wait. My curiosity tripped happily onto a less serious path.

"Bad hair day?" I asked, expecting her to laugh and caution me against napping with a damp head.

Instead, she chewed her lip and proved ominously silent.

"Jewel?" Dad asked carefully. "Is something wrong?"

"Yes," she answered, disaster in her tone.

My father's complexion turned the color of school paste. Seeing his horrified reaction, Jewel sputtered, "No. Yes. I mean, oh . . . I'm not dying." She dropped her scarf-covered head onto her arms, hiding her face.

I cast a sideways glance at Dad. He gave me a look that suggested we tread carefully.

Jewel said something inaudible. Her voice couldn't escape her position.

"What?" I asked.

"I said, 'I almost wish I were,' " Jewel cried.

This was not typical behavior for Jewel Johnson. Miss Johnson, the woman who had tamed hordes of high school home economics students. The woman who had shown the muffler man exactly how to replace a tail pipe.

Dad worked a silence as well as I. We waited, offering Jewel whatever space she needed. Eventually, she peeked over her arm. She moaned.

"I might as well show you," she said at last, sniffing away a final threatening tear. Timorously, she removed the scarf.

Initially I couldn't detect anything in her coiffeur that

might have birthed such a reaction. Then she lifted her face to meet my dad's.

I watched him extinguish a twinkle in his eye, but not swiftly enough.

"Go ahead," Jewel said, shaking her head. "Laugh. Get it over with. You wouldn't have found it so funny if you'd have seen me when my throat was closing up."

"Your throat?" I asked, trying not to stare. I gave up the fight. Jewel's chestnut bob, which had been graciously accommodating an increasing number of gray hairs, no longer supported any gray. In its place a lovely pink shone around the brown. Her temples proved particularly rose-colored.

Jewel nodded vigorously. "I think I was allergic to the hair dye. All of a sudden, my head itched and my throat felt funny. I rinsed my hair as quickly as I could . . ."

She placed her hand, with the scarf bunched in her fingers, at her temple. "All I could think of was that I was going to die. In an act of vanity. They'd find me cold, half-naked on the floor, a victim of dye death."

That was it. My father burst out laughing. He laughed until he hunched over and threatened tò choke up a lung. Charli felt moved to check on him. I tried not laughing. It proved impossible.

"I was wrong," Jewel said, standing and pacing our kitchen. "I'm going to die now. Humiliation will fell me like a collapsed soufflé."

Her distress urged Dad and I to rein in our laughter.

"You've always looked well in pink," my father said, attempting reason. He failed. A fresh outpouring of laughter doubled him over again.

Jewel caught her reflection in the metal handle of the refrigerator door.

"I am sadly reminded of *Anne of Green Gables* who so longed for her red hair to be a nice mahogany." Jewel sighed. "I figured that if I were going to rinse the gray, I might as well add a bold splash of color. A bit of red. I got a bit of strawberry instead.''

"It's not that noticeable," I said truthfully. Unless you were looking at it.

Jewel plastered a smile on. "The good news is that it's not permanent. The bad news is that the new improved formula is supposed to last twenty-eight washings. I figure if I wash it twice a day I only have two more weeks to endure it.''

She poked at the hair by her temples with her fingers. ". . . and the rest of my life to live it down.''

My father stood and walked to her, arms extended. She accepted the hug, laying her head gratefully on his shoulder.

"Are you sure that you won't be embarrassed to be seen with a dyed hussy?'' Jewel asked.

Dad winked at me over her head. "I'd be honored to be seen with you if your hair was purple. My Jewel. My beautiful, wonderful Jewel.''

"You're a pink zirconia," I suggested cheerfully.

They returned my suggestion with a glare.

"It looks fun," I tried again. "If you'd like, I could talk to Shari at the Ultimate Cut. I could ask her confidentially whether there was anyway we could touch it up.''

"Could you?" Jewel said, turning to me. She and Dad left their arms secured around each other's waists. "I'd surely appreciate it. Honestly, I don't know what got into me. I received an invitation to my cousin Zelda's wedding . . . you remember Zelda. She's my cousin in New Jersey.''

Jewel's face scrunched in a puzzled expression. "The next thing I knew, I was face-to-face with an aisle of hair coloring. They had more flavors than the gelatin aisle.''

Dad looked uncomfortable, nearly squirming. As I stood to clear the table, I wondered whether he'd surmised the origin of Jewel's impulse as I had. If so, let him squirm.

Jewel left Dad and began stowing the rest of the pie in

a plastic carrier. My father went to the sink and began running dish water.

"So Jewel," Dad said, drizzling dish soap in the path of the tap water. "What's the scoop about Gertrude Trent?"

I bent to return Charli's bowl to its corner out of the main traffic area, while Jewel wiped crumbs off the table.

Dad had moved to Landview in the early 1950s; Jewel was a native. Through her years at the high school and her mother's friendly nature, Jewel knew quite a few of the residents of our town.

"I'm trying to remember." Jewel sat again. "Where did you say she lived?"

"Tree Town," I replied, using the neighborhood's nickname. Since all its short blocks were named after trees, locals called the area Tree Town.

"Isn't that near the forest preserve? It's a bit secluded, isn't it?" Jewel replied, sitting back at the table.

I walked to the wall calendar, which hung beside the phone, and stared at the red star Dad had drawn on May 1, two short weeks from now. Momentarily, the murder was eclipsed by the Event. My recently consumed dessert curdled in my stomach like bad milk. I wondered *again* how I could have allowed myself to agree to such folly yet another time in this life.

"Yeah," Dad answered, stowing rinsed dishes in the dishwasher. He apparently hadn't registered my near-zombie behavior or my preoccupation with the calendar.

"Trent," Jewel mumbled. "Trent. That name is familiar. But I can't seem to place it. How old is Gertrude?"

"Good question." I pushed the future aside and leaned against the wall. I really didn't know that much about my latest client other than that her proposition had been irresistible.

Only the prospect of liquidating such a fascinating estate, coupled with Gertrude's assurances that she wasn't in a hurry to proceed, would have compelled me to take on a new job a mere two weeks before my first art exhibition in nearly four years. It was just my luck that Guy Tortelli would turn up in cold storage, catapulting this job from the arena of professional challenge into gold-medal distraction.

I felt akin to those split personality types. Part of me wished to do nothing except finish my latest oil painting. Part of me wanted to midwife my fledgling estate sale business into its next phase of growth. And the always-unpredictable part of me longed to chuck the other two roles and sleuth.

"How old did you say Gertrude was?" Jewel repeated.

I'm terrible at guessing ages. "I think she's probably between sixty and eighty."

"That narrows it down tremendously, Katie," my father said, wiping his hands on a checked towel. "She'd be born somewhere between 1917 and 1937."

"I know that her mother owned the house and her grandmother before her," I added, a bit defensively.

"I detect an absence of men," Dad quipped, pinching a dead blossom off an African violet by the window.

"We have Guy Tortelli," I suggested.

"Had," he corrected.

"Had."

The three of us silently searched our memories. I tried to think of anything I might have seen in the house which would reveal Gertrude's background. I came up confused.

"I used to 'cut' a man named Trent back in the early days at the shop," Dad said at last. "He sported impressive muttonchop sideburns, ruddy complexion, and a burn scar on his neck, the shape of a crescent. Not too chatty. Good tipper. He worked for the railroad."

"That would be Jethro Trent," Jewel said, nodding. "His wife volunteered at the hospital with my mother. She substituted occasionally for their Wednesday bridge club."

Jewel fell silent. A smile teased the corner of her mouth.

"You remember something," I said, loving the delicious lick of successful detection stroking my spine.

"Maybe."

"Okay, darling," Dad said, claiming a seat beside her. "Don't be a dyed-hussy tease. What's the scoop?"

It wasn't often that Jewel had the lead in one of our little clue hunts. She took her time answering. When she did, I could see why she appeared so self-satisfied.

Chapter Six

"Gertrude Trent worked for the State Department?" I repeated.

"Yes. Very hush-hush. She was the Trents' only child and after she went off to college, she sort of disappeared." Jewel's face was alive with interest. Her delight in helping had totally dismissed her former self-consciousness about her hair. "There was the usual gossip and speculation. I think that's what finally drove her mother . . . what was her name? . . . something with an 'L' . . ."

Jewel drummed her fingers on the table. I knew better than to interrupt her.

"Loretta. That's it. Loretta Trent."

Charli decided that he'd been ignored long enough. He stood at the door and offered a single bark, which sounded remarkably like "out."

"Just a minute, boy," Dad said. He leaned toward Jewel. "You were saying?"

"Well, one day her mother sort of let it slip that Gertrude had this special job, that's why she was gone so much. She showed the bridge club ladies a letter she'd gotten from Gertrude on White House stationery. Promised everyone not to tell."

Charli interrupted. *"Oouuut."*

"Hold on," Dad told him.

The dog began pacing agitatedly from Dad to the door.

"My mother didn't exactly believe her. Neither did any of the other ladies. They all figured Gertie had gotten her-

47

self in trouble. Maybe even that Loretta believed the story that she'd made up.''

''Gertie?'' I asked. Picturing the vast selection of international goods in Gertrude's home, I could swallow the bit about the State Department. That anyone would have the nerve to call the imposing Gertrude ''Gertie'' stretched my imagination.

Charli began singing, a baying lament for the outdoors.

''Okay, already,'' Dad said, standing. He traipsed to the back door and let Charli out to the attached screen porch. After checking the yard for squirrels, he opened the storm door and let the dog outside.

''She probably was some kind of secretary. I doubt if she were involved in anything really interesting,'' Dad said, scratching his neck.

I thought of that lithograph of the Green Room and wasn't so sure.

It took a while for the pounding on the front door the next morning to penetrate my sleep. For a moment, I thought I was still painting. The booming was the nature-sounds CD I had run continuously to keep me centered on ''The Storm,'' my work in progress.

The banging continued as I pried open my right eye.

I'd fallen asleep in the second bedroom, the one I'd converted to a studio, at some ridiculously late hour. In the cruel morning light, I discovered that my urgent indigo and navy strokes had failed to convey the intensity that I'd imagined the night before.

Groaning, I pulled the pillow over my head, hoping that the early riser at the door would go away. Possibly when I emerged, my painting wouldn't be completely awful either.

A persistent snout nudged me under the arm.

''Go away, Charli,'' I told the dog. ''I'm attempting performance art. This is a study in anguish.''

His cold nose connected with my armpit.

"Better yet," I told him, as I grew more awake, "why don't you go answer the door?"

Charli padded away, his nails clicking agreeably on the hardwood stairs. Tossing the pillow against the wall, I stretched. I detest self-pity. Having allowed myself a full five minutes, I was now finished. Leaning on my elbows, I examined the seven completed paintings spread across the walls of the modest room.

A smile, which was a sweet mixture of relief and pride, rose to my lips. They were good. They were very good.

I shoved my hair out of my face. Maybe the exhibition wouldn't be a fiasco. Certainly there was something of destiny about the way the whole affair had come about.

Suddenly, I heard something that I never thought to hear in my house, in my dad's house.

I drew my knees to my chest and stared openmouthed at the doorway. I'd fallen asleep in one of Dad's sleeveless undershirts and a pair of shamrock-patterned boxer shorts. My flannel painting shirt lay tossed across a wooden chair in the corner. I wasn't dressed for company.

Charli hustled back into the room, moments before Gertrude Trent appeared framed in my doorway like a stately Austrian expatriate. I'd little time to admire her cape, hat, and boots.

"You didn't answer, but the dog let me in," she said, not batting an eye at my eccentric attire.

I reminded myself to thank Dad for teaching Charli to open the storm door *and* for leaving the entry door ajar.

"Gertrude," I said, finding my voice. "What are you doing here?"

She offered a pleased grin. "We've a case to crack. I wanted to be sure we got some results before the local cops bungle anything."

As though she thought nothing peculiar in getting me out of bed, she began circling the room, examining my work. "Get yourself decent," she told me, stopping and squinting in front of "Ella's Project," the first in the series. "I'll treat myself to a private showing." She offered a low whistle. "And, quite the treat it is."

I couldn't help flushing with pride as I rose from the bed. Casting the bed coverings hastily in place, I wondered at Gertrude's determination. Again, given the proper incentive, she'd scaled another set of stairs.

"I assume you have a destination, a plan in mind?" I called from the bathroom. The words bubbled around my toothpaste and toothbrush.

"Of course," Gertrude called back. "When's the exhibition?"

I paused, my hand on the shower faucet. Having told her nothing about my art career, I wondered at her conclusion. Obviously the woman knew an art studio when she saw it, but why would she deduce an imminent showing?

As though she'd taken my silence for a question, Gertrude went on. "I see a fine selection of professional paintings, a printout of addresses, which I assume are for invitations, and a wastebasket overflowing with spent cola slushes. Deduction: a nervous artist on the verge."

I ran the water into the tub over her Sherlock Holmes bit. She'd gotten the nervous part right.

"I'll be out in a minute," I yelled. Gertrude might be accustomed to calling the shots. However, I went nowhere without my morning shower. She'd just have to sit tight.

By the time I'd emerged from the bathroom, all clean and spiffy, Gertrude had made herself comfortable in a worn plaid recliner tucked beside the daybed.

"Gertrude?" I asked, approaching gently. She looked as though she might have been sleeping.

"Good," she cried. Her eyes flung open. Dropping the footrest with a bang and letting the chair rock her forward,

Gertrude straightened her cap with her wrist. "The chase, Kathryn," she said, rising, "is on."

I swept down the stairs before her, tying an indigo-and-purple scarf splashed with gold stars around my forehead as a hair band. My hand-painted "mystic" kimono and palazzo pants felt light and airy. Turning at the foot of the stairs, I prepared to catch her, though it would be impossible, if she might stumble. More likely, I'd be crushed beneath her not-petite form.

"Would you like me to drive?" I asked, as she reached my side by the open door.

Past a steadying breath, Gertrude gestured at my Good Buys van with her cane. "Stealth is required," she answered. "I'll drive."

Charli waited expectantly. He always seems to know when something's afoot.

"Does he generally join you?" Gertrude asked, nodding at the dog.

"He likes to be the wheel man, but he's too heavy on the gas pedal for my taste."

"Fine," she answered. "Let him be backup. Come on, Charli."

The dog capered outside and met us at Gertrude's "unobtrusive vehicle." We might have drawn less attention to ourselves in my van!

As Gertrude careened around corners, I wondered if she'd gone to the same driving school as Jewel. There were distinct similarities in their style, I thought as my scarf rippled out the open window. Her gray vintage Mercedes handled like a thoroughbred. Gertrude appeared to delight in "giving it its head."

"The last time Guy was here, he had a nasty toothache," Gertrude explained, over the sound of the wind pouring through the windows. She seemed to enjoy the breeze in her face as much as I. Charli, with his head out the window, was in doggy paradise. "I sent him to my dentist. If my suspicions are correct," she went on, crossing town with abandon, "the dentist will have X rays of Guy's teeth."

"And we'll be that much closer to knowing for sure if Guy Tortelli was Cameron Kordell," I finished for her, resting my hand on Charli's collar.

"Precisely," Gertrude answered, a smile making her face an eager portrait of age and vivacity.

If Gertrude were making a pretense of investigating Tortelli's demise, she was doing an exceptional job. I detected nothing in her behavior but the vital joy of a capable woman finally assigned a worthy task.

Dr. Turnbin's practice thrived in a made-over turn-of-the-century Painted Lady. A neat wood sign in the coral, forget-me-knot blue, and champagne colors of the Victorian home served as his shingle.

We bypassed the handicapped parking place and stowed the Mercedes among the fleet of suburban vehicles wedged in the narrow lot.

"Nice," I commented as we passed a tan flagstone-lined flower bed bursting with short red tulips.

"Professional job," Gertrude sniffed, implying that any landscaping farmed out to others was tainted in some way, nouveau riche.

The quaint, inviting front porch and unobtrusive oak ramp gave way to a waiting room full of patients and a sterile, glassed-in reception area. It offered as much warmth as an ice pack.

Gertrude strode briskly forward.

When a medium-sized woman with a severe ash permanent failed to acknowledge us, Gertrude rapped smartly on the glass with the head of her cane.

The receptionist looked up, displaying a prim button mouth and too much blue eye shadow. Purposefully finishing what she was doing, the lady then skimmed over to us.

"Have you signed in?" she asked, squinting at us.

If I didn't know better, I'd have read censure in her glance. She didn't care for our looks. Imagine.

"No, we—" I began.

"You have to sign in," the woman interrupted nastily. She passed us a clipboard through a slot designed for such exchanges. "If your mother can't fill out the form herself, you'll have to do it for her."

I felt Gertrude bristle beside me.

"Young woman," Gertrude said, pulling out her pocket notebook. "What is your name?" Her pen remained poised above the open page, ready to enter this upstart on her almighty list.

"I am not obliged to give you that information."

I'd seen Marines more easily intimidated than this woman.

"Now," the lady continued, "you need to take this form and step aside. I have other work to do."

"Sharpening your claws?" Gertrude muttered, not quite loudly enough for the other lady to overhear. "Kathryn, there are petty bureaucrats in this world. And there are *mean,* petty bureaucrats. We've got us a mean one."

"You," Gertrude called out, striking the glass again. "Ms. Obliged. Please tell Dr. Turnbin that Gertrude Trent is here to see him."

Gertrude managed to maintain her authoritative manner despite the other lady's superior reply. "Dr. Turnbin is on vacation. Dr. Jessup is filling in. Dr. Jessup is with patients."

I drew a deep breath. This was getting us nowhere.

"Ma'am," I said, drawing on my finest schoolgirl voice. "Please don't mind my aunt, she's a little off. If you know what I mean."

Gertrude scowled at both of us. The receptionist pursed her lips even tighter.

"I'm sure that *you* can help me. It's obvious that you're

in charge here," I added, hoping to finish this bit before I choked on my own performance. "I'm afraid that her son, my cousin, Guy Tortelli, has had a terrible accident. Yes, a garbage truck collided with his moped. Miraculously, he walked away without a scratch. And then, dazed as he was, he walked smack into a brick wall. Broke his nose and damaged his teeth. You know, those two pointy ones and the big front ones."

I poked inside my mouth to demonstrate.

Gertrude, taking her cue from me, now appeared more distracted by concern than angry. The receptionist remained incredulous.

I sped on. "We've hired an excellent plastic surgeon and an oral surgeon, but it would be very helpful if we could have Guy's old X rays so that the reconstruction is faithful."

"A wall, you say?"

"Please," I rushed on. "I'd be so grateful." Very grateful, to get out of here and away from this unpleasant woman.

She paused as though considering my request. I turned to Gertrude.

"This was the date of his last visit," Gertrude said, slipping a paper with Guy's full name and the date of his emergency appointment written on it, to the receptionist.

"This is five years ago," the receptionist said. "Has he seen Dr. Turnbin since then? We don't keep retired records in here." She gestured at the horizontal file cabinets lining the room.

"What do you do with them?" Gertrude inquired, tired of acting infirm.

"They're stored in the basement. By year. Alphabetically." She squinted her eyes at us. "I couldn't possibly go and search through them now."

"But," I said, pleading. "What about Guy's overbite?

He's famous for that look—just like David Letterman. We need those X rays!''

''Oh, Kathryn,'' Gertrude cried suddenly, her free hand moving absently to her chest. ''Kathryn.''

She buckled over against me. If Gertrude were to suffer some horrible attack because of this beastly receptionist, I didn't know what I'd do. As rage mixed with fear poured through me, Gertrude clutched my arm.

''My pills,'' she gasped. ''I need my pills.''

''Shall I call the paramedics?'' the receptionist asked, suddenly alarmed.

''No!'' Gertrude cried.

''Where are your pills?'' I asked.

She drew me close. ''In the basement,'' she hissed. ''Head for the basement and get that file.''

I glanced into her shining, red face. She winked at me.

The receptionist had emerged from her glass enclave to help steer Gertrude into an empty seat in the waiting room. I took the opportunity to speed down the hall, to where an open stairwell suggested the basement.

Kathryn, I told myself, whisking down the stairs, *she's loony, and you're double loony for following her lead.*

Flicking on an overhead fluorescent light, I discovered that the basement was lined with old metal shelving. Crates and crates of files lingered down here among the whitewashed walls. I checked the contents of the nearest crate. *Abbot, retired 1945.* How long had this Turnbin been practicing dentistry, anyway?

Taking in the vast room, I bit back a curse. There was no way I'd be able to find a single file in a hurry. We'd have to come up with another plan.

As I clambered back up the stairs, I could hear that Gertrude's show hadn't closed yet.

''Here, Auntie,'' I said, pressing my way past the good Samaritans. I drew a square white tablet out of a pocket of my backpack. ''Take this.''

Gertrude's eyes flared for a moment at the size of the "pill." Nevertheless, she accepted it, stowing it under her tongue.

"What's going on in here?" an unctuous male voice bellowed. "Mrs. Offenheimer, I am attempting to perform a root canal!"

The substitute dentist had appeared in the hallway. Gloved and masked, he held some kind of scalpel.

"I'm sorry, Doctor," Offenheimer stammered. "These women—"

It was my turn to interrupt.

"Oh, Doctor," I cried, pressing toward him. "We need an old file from your basement. Auntie became ill trying to convince your receptionist of the urgency of our situation."

I tossed my scarf over my shoulder and flashed him my pearly whites. "You see my cousin Guy was struck . . ."

"Offenheimer," he said, apparently not impressed by me at all. "Get this woman what she wants and see that I get what I want—a peaceful, working atmosphere!"

"Yes, Doctor."

As the receptionist disappeared into the basement, I almost felt sorry for her. Good graces were obviously confined to this building itself. Its occupants were quite testy.

I returned to Gertrude who, mission accomplished, was beginning to look more robust. She was firmly informing a pushy young man wearing a Maid for You uniform, "No. I do not need CPR. You only require CPR when you are technically dead. I am not dead yet."

My reappearance sent her would-be savior back to his mop and bucket. He was either terribly interested in CPR or mighty disappointed at Gertrude's resiliency. The tight set of his shoulders and the hostile look in his eyes did not seem those of a natural healer.

Against my will, I wanted to hug her. She'd given me a

fright earlier. In that moment, I'd discovered how much I'd grown to care for her.

The receptionist returned with a file, and a release form, which I filled out as "Joan Collins."

We made our escape with the file beneath Gertrude's cape and her leaning on my arm.

"What was that you gave me back there?" Gertrude asked as we maneuvered to her car.

"Chiclet," I answered.

"Not bad," she replied, chewing happily.

Gertrude allowed me to drive, making me wonder whether a bit of her performance might have been genuine.

"Where are you headed?" she asked, holding the X rays to the light as though she knew how to read them.

"Phase two," I told her. We had Guy Tortelli's X rays. Now we needed a baseline for comparison. There was only one way that I could think of to get X rays for Cameron Kordell.

I hoped Gertrude didn't mind clutter, because our next destination personified the word.

Chapter Seven

Gertrude warily eyed the establishment. One of the things I was enjoying about working with her was her keen intellect. She didn't inquire why I'd parked before ReRead, the paperback book exchange; she merely stated, "I had thought we'd go to the library."

"This will be quicker," I replied, holding the door open for Charli to bound out. "I'm sure they'll have multiple copies of all of Kordell's novels. We'll put them on my father's account."

ReRead crouched in one of those strip malls built in the early sixties, which now appeared as dated as greased pompadours. I held the heavy entry door open for Gertrude as she attempted squeezing past one of the stacks of boxed books, which awaited the owner's attention by the door.

Gertrude sniffed and peered around the store. It was spilling over with novels on shelves, novels in cardboard boxes, and tottering piles of novels thigh high.

Charli scampered past a center carousel, which hawked half-price new books. He wagged his way enthusiastically to a woman who was attempting to hang an advertising poster for a book entitled *Wild Rider*. The glossy photo featured a splendid rifleman, sans shirt, astride a trumpeting stallion.

A simple nose nudge had the lady squealing.

"Charli!" She laughed, a sound not unlike a tommy gun giving birth. "Wha-wha-what a tre-tre-treat. Look who's here, Clarrrrrice. Charli."

An apple dumpling of a woman quit inventorying romances and grumbled something like, "Just what we need. Fleas and paw prints to spruce the place up."

"Hello, Clarice," I called, accustomed to her sour mood. I couldn't blame her. The woman tried desperately to bring some measure of cleanliness to the owner's apparent chaos. Not to be.

"Hello, Sonia," I said, as the stuttering owner of ReRead caught me in a quick embrace. "Great glasses."

Sonia's latest bit of eyewear proved to be flowing, pink plastic butterfly-shaped frames. The pink rhinestones dotting the edges matched the jangle of sparkling earrings that hung nearly to her shoulders from each earlobe.

"This is my client, Gertrude Trent," I went on. "Gertrude, Sonia Hill, the owner of ReRead."

"Ppppleased to me-e-e-et you." Sonia flashed a smile as dazzling as her glasses.

"My pleasure," Gertrude replied, offering a firm handshake. "Interesting place you have here."

Clarice grumbled something about "fire hazards and fruitcakes" before she disappeared into the stacks.

"Clever name for the establishment," Gertrude added.

"I thought so," Sonia said, nudging a stray paperback under a folding table with the toe of her Birkenstocks. "Stuuuttering. Reeeeading. ReReading. It fit."

Gertrude laughed heartily.

"A ch-ch-chair." Sonia looked around. "Would you like to sit?" She produced a chair that might comfortably accommodate a four-year-old. "No. Heavens. No. Sillllly me."

"I'm fine," Gertrude said, keeping Sonia from trashing any more of her store in an attempt to be hospitable.

"We came to get some books," I said. "Do you have any of Cameron Kordell's novels?"

Sonia smirked. "O-o-one or two."

Charli traipsed after her as she disappeared into the back of the store.

"How does she keep an inventory of all this?" Gertrude asked, nodding at the close spaces.

"In her head," I replied. "Drives Clarice crazy."

Proving my point, Sonia reappeared with Charli in tow. Her arms were loaded with books. She deposited them unceremoniously beside the register.

"*Sparkle, Neon, Fortune, Billboard . . .*" I held up a smaller ragged volume. "What's this one?"

Clarice showed up in time to reply, "That's one of his earlier books. Before he wrote the glitz, he'd sold a couple of Regency romances under the name Grace Cameron."

Picking up the worn book, Gertrude studied the cover. "Looks like we came to the right place, Kathryn. You all certainly know your literature."

Sonia beamed with pleasure. Clarice flared her nostrils, saying, "We are booksellers, after all."

"Of course," I said.

While Clarice rang up our purchase, Sonia brought out her special stash of doughnut holes. I passed. Gertrude and Charli ate a few.

"Cooome again," Sonia said, attempting to beat us to the door and tripping over her own feet.

"It would be my pleasure," Gertrude said sincerely.

Charli barked once.

"I'll get the door," I told Sonia. "Thanks again."

From the sidewalk outside, I detected Clarice screaming at Sonia about city animal ordinances and underpricing. The last thing we heard was Sonia calling, "Yaaak, yaaaak. Yaaaak. Stifle, Clarice."

As we drove back across town, Gertrude flipped through the books in her lap.

"Kathryn," she said, as though she'd only just thought

of it. "Pull over up there. We might as well get a cup of java while we pick through these."

My eyes darted to the right. Was she pulling my leg? Had she noticed my determinedly bypassing Landview's newest business, Convivium?

"I'll make you a cup at my house," I answered, hoping to dissuade her. My first visit to Convivium, a gem of a coffeehouse, had completely altered my life path.

"I'd rather drink Drāno," she answered. "Come on, Kathryn." Gertrude gazed out the window at the made-over brownstone. Sleek, contemporary light fixtures and bold plantings separated the older building from its neighbors. "I've heard the place has possibilities."

I was learning the futility of quibbling with her. Pulling into the lot, which was fairly empty at this time of day, I willed my heart to a steady beat.

"You stay here," I told Charli as I exited the car. The owner did not like dogs. I still hadn't figured out how Charli was going to attend the showing. Dad was vociferous that the entire family must be there.

Glancing up at the spectacular rehab the owner had done, anticipation again ran laps through my belly. I could imagine the parking lot bursting with patrons. Divine decor, tantalizing refreshments—

"Besides," Gertrude said, interrupting my reverie. "I want to see where your exhibition is going to be."

"My—How did you know?" I asked.

She laughed heartily and swung herself solidly up the curved, broad path. "I read about it in the *South Sub Gazette.* You're to be the first artist showing at the quote 'oh-so-tony Convivium—where like-minded souls nourish themselves on all levels' unquote."

I groaned. Notoriety had never been my favorite playmate. The last time I'd attempted to seduce the public with my art, Gary had been beside me, ostensibly supporting me and unfortunately undermining me.

"Never fear, Kathryn," Gertrude proclaimed, choosing the support of the iron railing and the few stairs over the length of the ramp. "Your work is exceptional. Time will proclaim you the talent that you are."

I paused with my hand on the brass door latch and stared at her. It occured to me that she might be trying to dazzle me with false praise, any tactic to prevent my investigating *her*.

"You are unaccustomed to compliments?" she asked, studying me intently.

My brow furrowed as the echo of former accolades called from the past but did not quite register.

"I think perhaps you were told them and possibly you disregarded them," Gertrude said, her voice kind, her expression gentle. "When someone is deaf, it doesn't matter how loud the world shouts."

She put her hand over mine. "I trust your hearing has improved with your art."

If her overtures of friendship were feigned, they still managed to penetrate my heart. "Come on," she said, "you can buy me a cappuccino."

I followed her inside. The aroma of freshly ground coffee beans hung dark and exotic in the air. The gleaming white plaster walls seemed pristine by contrast—a tabula rasa for new experience. The unadorned crown moldings and pillars joining the marblized tile lent dimension to the open-concept main floor level.

Teak bistro-style tables were scattered around the open staircase, which led to the second floor. Danish upholstered furniture formed cozy conversation pits in the immediate two dining areas. Across the room, a converted porch boasted flowing green ferns and outdoor furniture that appeared more expensive than my indoor stuff.

Several women spoke in quiet tones at a table near the front window. One nursed a teacup the size of half a cantaloupe.

"This will do nicely," Gertrude said, stepping into the west room with the air of an inspector.

It was more than nice, I thought. It was fabulous. I could see my paintings adorning these classic walls. Excitement set my jittery nerves singing. Things were going to be perfect. I had nothing to worry about.

As though Kareem, the owner, had sensed our arrival, I heard his distinctive voice approaching from the kitchen.

Last fall, when Jewel had insisted we sample the new coffeehouse wares, I had not suspected that the owner would be Kareem Duane Williams, a dear friend from the fine arts department at Illinois University Northwest. Kareem couldn't believe that I'd stopped pursuing my serious art. One thing had led to another. Between Jewel and Kareem I'd been signed to be his first exhibition before I had known what hit me.

"I'm absolutely blown away, I tell you. This is too, too far out." Kareem spoke boisterously to an unseen companion.

Gertrude, deducing Kareem's identity, remained standing, awaiting his arrival and an introduction.

I smiled, drawing a grateful deep breath. Convivium was aptly named. Kareem had created an atmosphere that was at once stimulating and relaxing, a hideaway designed to invite relationships and nurture beauty.

"Kareem," I said happily, as he entered the room.

"Kathryn," he replied, his voice pitched higher in surprise. His dusky eyes darted from me to Gertrude to the person coming up behind him.

"Kathryn?" a hauntingly familiar voice asked eagerly.

As a tall man pressed past Kareem, I felt my eyes sort of glaze over as my smile wilted. The sharp pain in my stomach, which had been manifesting increasingly, drew my attention.

"Gary?" I replied, gulping.

I hate surprises.

*   *   *

That evening Charli and I took a long walk. We traipsed over to the undeveloped field abutting the expressway. I let him tear around the pseudo-prairie while I picked my way over the uneven ground avoiding snake holes and bogs.

"Gary. Gary." I couldn't stop repeating his name to myself as though its taste on my tongue would render this afternoon less vivid.

The four of us had shared a nauseatingly civilized repast of scones and coffee. Gary, who had gotten wind of the exhibition, had surprised Kareem by dropping by only minutes before our arrival. The ex-love of my life, the next Ansel Adams, was currently thriving as a computer salesman. He was thrilled to hear of my rebirth. After all, he'd always had the utmost faith in my talent, he reiterated.

I tripped over a chunk of concrete jutting out of the muck.

"Shoot," I said, barely avoiding an expletive. Pain shot past my Nikes. "Shoot, shoot, shoot," I repeated, limping along. Where was Charli anyway? If he came back with a dead carcass, I'd kill him.

Pausing, I attended myself to the roar of the expressway ahead and the evening chatter of hidden insects. How was I supposed to focus on my showing with Gary hovering about, the Trent sale, and Guy Tortelli's murder investigation?

An early mosquito nipped my cheek. I slapped it forcefully.

After the Convivium reunion, Gertrude and I had pored over the acknowledgments and publishing info of the books we'd gotten at ReRead. She was savvy enough to ignore my bad humor and allow me the grace of losing myself in the process.

To My Wife, Theresa. With gratitude to my agent, Richard Lambert. Hearts and Flames Romance.

The books had proven a gold mine of information about

Cameron Kordell, aka Grace Cameron. Now all we had to do was contact some of the folks mentioned in the author notes and try verifying if Guy Tortelli was in fact Cameron Kordell. Gertrude had said something about making a few calls tonight.

By that time, a headache had loomed so powerfully behind my eyes that I had felt nauseated.

"So here I am," I said, tearing off a spent milkweed pod. "A bath, a couple of Tylenol, and three cola slushes later. Vertical, healthy, and utterly confused."

Charli burst through some bramble, his tongue lolling stupidly from his mouth. His eyes shone bright with the unexpected freedom I'd given him. He seemed to share none of my misgivings about the grooming he'd need later, or my emotional turmoil.

"You've never met Gary," I told the dog. He cocked his ears at me. "He's aged with annoying grace. I'd forgotten what a husky voice he had."

Charli and I continued our hike, with him beside me now.

"At least I didn't make a complete idiot out of myself and accept his dinner invitation." I tossed the milkweed into a stand of hawthorn, startling a rabbit into flight. Charli sped away in eager pursuit.

"Go ahead," I called after him. "Leave. Why should you be any different?"

Different, different, different . . . My words echoed back to me. I'd reached the cavernous underbelly of the expressway. As traffic droned above, the ground literally vibrated with the energy of so many people driving so quickly to anywhere else.

Had I felt abandoned by Gary? I'd been the one to break off our relationship. How could that be?

Gang graffiti peppered the ashen concrete supports of the

viaduct. I felt like a gnat inside a whale's belly. Diminished and vulnerable. Inexplicably, I thought of my mother.

Somehow my mother had always made me feel safe. In a household dominated by a drunken father, my sweet mother had proven a safe harbor. And then, she was gone.

The trucks thundering overhead became marauding death machines. Piloted by sleepy, intoxicated drivers. Men who should have pulled into some cheap hotel and slept it off. Men who, instead, broadsided my mother's car, killing her instantly.

Traffic grew deafening. A scream rose in my throat.

I swallowed it hard, until a knot of grief threatened to choke me.

"Charli!" I yelled, unleashing a demon of emotion in my call. "Charli!"

Chapter Eight

Gertrude greeted me at 8:30 that night as though she'd been expecting me. She was wearing something that looked like men's pajamas—pinstriped, breast pocket, buttons on the left side. A pair of half-reading glasses hung on her bosom.

"Kathryn," she said. "Do come in. I was just having a Postum. Grew accustomed to the stuff at the PX in Berlin. Would you care for a cup?"

"Sure," I said, "Why not?" It couldn't taste any worse than tea. I followed her into the house, tossing my safari hat on the sideboard. *The PX in Berlin?*

"Flying solo tonight?" Gertrude asked as she made her way to the kitchen.

"Charli wasn't presentable. His coat was a flora festival," I answered, discovering that Gertrude hadn't been merely sipping a nightcap. The books we'd bought, plus notebooks, a portable phone, and a laptop-plus-fax machine had turned the kitchen table into a working desk.

"You've snagged a bit yourself," she said, picking a dead leaf off my sleeve.

"Sorry," I mumbled, running my hand through my loose hair, hoping not to dislodge anything living.

"Think nothing of it," she answered, indicating a chair. "I've never been a fussy housekeeper. Never cared much for babies either. I suppose that's one reason why I found it difficult imagining myself as a wife and mother."

"You never married?" I asked, accepting the cup of Postum. It smelled like four-year-old coffee.

"I had plenty of offers." She'd sat and seemed to be viewing the past in the glossy surface of her drink. "One regret. Had I a chance to do things over . . ." Her voice trailed off. She shook her head. Her expression sharpened. She pinned me with a look.

"I assume your evening visit has something to do with that Gary fellow," she said, rubbing the ceramic surface of her mug as though it might coax the truth out of me.

We shared a long, knowing look. In the depths of her eyes lay a kindred spirit, an invitation to share, a wealth of wisdom. No hint of deceit.

"I'd rather talk about this," I said truthfully, sweeping my hand over her working area.

"Certainly," she answered amiably. Her voice grew enthusiastic. "It was easy enough to get phone numbers for the publishing companies Kordell had worked with. I've discovered that his agent, Richard Lambert, is still active. Handles mostly midlist authors as far as I can tell. I'm waiting for a call on the wife, or more likely, ex-wife."

"My bet," I said, "is that they're divorced. It's hard to imagine a wife tolerating his extended visits to you, or that she wouldn't have at least reported him missing."

"If Kordell is Tortelli," Gertrude pointed out.

"Do you doubt it?"

"No," she answered. "It fits. We still need to prove it though."

I felt better already. There was nothing like an absorbing bit of homicide to take your mind off your worries. As I was entertaining a smidgin of guilt at finding such respite in a dead man, Gertrude's fax machine began receiving.

She drew the single sheet of paper from the machine and donned her reading glasses. Chuckling, she said, "Colin was always such a joker."

Colin? I attempted to discern any identifying marks on the fax.

"Don't strain yourself, Kathryn," Gertrude said, passing me the fax. "I called in a few favors."

In my hands was a disturbingly professional report on not only Theresa Tortelli, but Guy Tortelli, aka Cameron Kordell. The CIA must have files on everyone, I thought, shuddering. Everything including Theresa's parent's names and Guy's attendance at Kent State demonstrations against the Vietnam War filled the pages.

"The CIA?" I asked, arching an eyebrow at her. "Somehow I hadn't imagined them as the friendly types."

Gertrude sipped her Postum. Her gray eyes glinted mischievously over the brim of her cup.

"I have a feeling that you have more secrets than Guy Tortelli did," I added.

She stood and went to the counter to mix herself another drink. "Let's just say," she replied, turning, "that I've enjoyed a full life."

"Care to elaborate?"

"I'd rather discuss the work at hand." *

Touché.

"It looks like we went to a lot of trouble to get those dental records for nothing. This report makes pretty clear that Guy Tortelli was Cameron Kordell," I said, reading the fax again.

"Yes," Gertrude said, swinging her cane and ambling back to the table with her drink. "But we had great fun, didn't we?"

I forced a disapproving look. "You frightened me at the dentist's. I was afraid you were really having some kind of medical emergency."

"I should be so lucky." Gertrude rubbed her hip meaningfully. "There are worse fates in this techno-medical world than sudden death. The prospect of lingering longevity frankly terrifies me."

Despite her handicap, I'd never thought of Gertrude as declining. I couldn't imagine her infirm.

"Anyway," she said brightly, sloughing off her confession, "tomorrow, we give the ex-wife a call."

"And the agent," I said, pushing aside my still-full Postum. "I'd like to know why he didn't pursue an investigation when such an important client came up missing."

"Indeed," Gertrude replied. She yawned and drew herself up. "Now go home. It's time that we both had some sleep."

A slim wedge of moon like a dieter's portion of cheese hung strangely in the dark night sky. A bad air day obscured what in the country might have been a blanket of stars. I could barely make out the North Star as I made my way down Gertrude's drive to where I'd parked on the street.

My step proved a good deal lighter than when I'd arrived. I had no idea when I'd taken on the Trent sale that it would prove so diverting. Gertrude was no criminal. I suspected that in Gertrude Trent I'd acquired more than a client, possibly a friend.

A copious lilac jutting around the corner of the lot dripped the promise of moist sweet blossom. As I ducked past a wayward branch, a man's voice pierced the evening quiet.

"Hold it right there."

Reacting instinctively, I spun and kicked, aiming my foot where I hoped it would do the most damage.

"Where did you learn that little maneuver?" Detective Cole asked, firmly entrapping my leg in his strong grasp. He yanked once, forcing me to hop closer and placing me in a horrifyingly vulnerable position with my leg on his hip. "The Angie Dickinson School of Dumb Defense?"

I didn't want to tell him that I'd picked up a self-defense video at one of our sales, nor that I'd only gotten through the first five minutes of it. His fingers on my calf proved unrelenting. His breath smelled of spearmint.

"Can I have my leg back?" I must have looked like a flamingo wrapped around him this way.

"Not yet. Were I an assailant, you can see how such an ill-advised kick would place you in a worse situation than you were already in." Cole's eyes didn't leave mine. I'd a feeling he might be enjoying my distress.

"I understand. Now can I have my leg back?"

"In a minute." He smiled slowly. "You and Ms. Trent have had a very busy day."

"How . . . ?"

"I had you followed. It seemed like the easiest way to keep tabs on your meddling."

My supporting leg began aching. I rested my hands on his shoulders and prepared to push hard if he didn't let go soon.

"Who was the man you met at Convivium?"

Did I detect more than professional interest?

When I didn't answer immediately, he said gruffly, "I'm not sure that I like you, Ms. Bogert."

Our entwined position suggested otherwise. Tipping my chin higher, I pulled back. "You're not?"

He shoved me away, lest he manifest any further proof of his ambivalence.

"So—did the autopsy confirm that Tortelli had been shot?" I asked.

"Nice try, Bogert," he answered, popping a coffee stirrer between his teeth. "I suggest we play it this way. Why does Gertrude Trent come up on the computers as a 'don't touch?' She has a security clearance that I've never even heard of."

"Did she?"

"Don't play dumb with me."

We walked along the chain-link together, maintaining a friendly distance. "Has it occurred to you that Ms. Trent might be responsible for Tortelli's cold storage? It *is* her house. He *was* her boarder. Have you considered that by helping her you could be playing into the hands of a calculating murderess?''

It had, until a few minutes ago. I knew in my gut that Gertrude hadn't murdered Tortelli.

"So he *was* murdered," I persisted doggedly.

"Maybe. Maybe not," Cole replied, sighing. "Death occurred from a blow to the back of the head. It might have been an accident."

"He didn't accidentally lock himself in the freezer though, did he?" I quipped.

"No. He didn't."

I'd begun wandering ahead, entertaining a multitude of theories about how the death blow might have occurred. Cole grabbed my wrist, halting me.

"I want you to butt out of this investigation. I want you to concentrate on your opening," he said gruffly.

Did the whole town know about the art showing?

While I rallied a response, a large sedan lunged and wove around the corner. Its approaching headlights nearly blinded me as it accelerated, straight at us.

Cole's back was to the street. He began turning at the sound of the car.

"Look out!" I cried, throwing my weight into him.

We crashed into the chain-link together, moments before the vehicle would have struck. The car jerked to a stop with its front end perched on the sidewalk.

"Are you all right?" Cole asked, pushing my hair back from my face.

I nodded, struggling for breath.

He stormed over to the driver's door. With one hand on his service revolver and the other waving his badge, he called, "Out of the car. Keep your hands where I can see them."

Chapter Nine

I stood back watching Cole do his cop thing. Before the driver could emerge from the car, a man got out on the passenger side. His white oxford, no tie, was unbuttoned at the neck.

"I'm sorry, officer," the guy said, running his hand across his designer cut, demonstrating an officious interference.

"Detective," Cole corrected. "Don't move." He managed to watch both men simultaneously. "Get out of the car," he told the driver.

I'd retrieved a flashlight from my backpack and shone it in the driver's face. The young man clutching the steering wheel appeared to be a younger, more acne-driven version of the man who was tentatively skirting the front of the car.

"Detective," the older guy said diplomatically. "Of course. I'm really sorry about this. Jerry Junior here just got his learner's permit and we were trying to get in some driving practice."

Jerry Junior's Adam's apple continued a tense journey up and down his scrawny neck.

"No real harm done, eh, off— . . . detective?"

"You are aware, sir," Cole said, "that a minor driving under your supervision is legally your responsibility."

"I am aware of the law, and I applaud you in your performance." He extended his hand. "I'm Jerry Ritter. Running for Congress. It will be my pleasure to advocate funding for such a diligent, understanding law enforcement community.''

I shot the light in his face. He winced, holding up his hand, which sported a diamond ring the size of that Chiclet I'd given Gertrude earlier.

''That might be construed as a bribe, Mr. Ritter,'' Cole replied carefully.

''Detective.'' Ritter leaned against the hood of his expensive car as he withdrew his snakeskin wallet. He handed it to Cole. A twenty-dollar bill tipped out of the billfold behind his driver's license. ''If I were to hand you something like this, hypothetically, that might be considered a bribe.

''But, if . . .'' He dropped a fifty on the ground. ''. . . I didn't notice that I'd dropped a bit of cash and you found it later, that would be a bit of luck on your part, wouldn't you say?''

Jerry Junior shook so badly behind the wheel that it was embarrassing. His father, on the other hand, reeked with an aura of smug control.

''Kathryn,'' Cole said, his voice rumbling and menacing as low thunder. ''Pick up the fifty.''

Stuffing the flashlight under my armpit, I stooped and grabbed the money.

''Now, give it to Mr. Ritter,'' Cole went on purposefully. ''He seems to have lost it.''

I stuffed the bill into the guy's shirt pocket. Cole stepped within a foot of Ritter, who stood tensely away from the car.

''Mr. Ritter,'' Cole said, ''you are lucky that I don't arrest you and your son. That wouldn't help the campaign much, would it?''

Jerry Junior groaned, dropping his forehead on the steering wheel with a clunk.

The would-be congressman seemed finally at a loss for words.

"Go home, Mr. Ritter," Cole said. "You drive."

"Thank you . . . detective. I appreciate your understanding. No hard feelings. Right?"

Cole didn't reply. He took me by the elbow. We stepped back so that the other two could change driving positions.

The last thing I saw of the Ritters, Jerry Senior was driving oh-so-carefully down the street and turning into the driveway of the placard-coated lawn.

"What a sleeze," I said, wondering why Cole had let him go.

"Either a sleeze or a moron," Cole replied. "I'll check him out."

"Everybody a suspect?"

"You're learning, Bogert. You're learning."

"Kathryn, wake up!"

Someone shook me, not gently. *What is it about this week?* I thought, flipping onto my belly, burying my face beneath my pillow. I *need* my eight hours.

"Go away," I grumbled. "Have some respect for the comatose."

"Oh, get on with you," Jewel said. "It's ten-thirty in the morning and time you got up."

"It is?" I groaned. What time had I fallen into bed last night? My circadian rhythms, never very reliable, seemed particularly erratic this week.

"It is," she answered, pulling up a chair beside me. "You've got to take better care of yourself, Kathryn," she said kindly. "I'm concerned that you're running yourself down between the showing and the case."

I tugged at the sheets constricting my right leg. I did not "run down" easily, possessing not only the bone structure but the stamina of a good horse.

"I've brought up some breakfast for you," Jewel said, reaching over and forcing one of my eyelids open. It took a moment for me to focus on her earnest face.

"Okay, okay," I said, shaking her hand away. "I'm awake. You, dear friend, will pay for this." I ran my tongue over my sleep-glazed teeth.

"I don't think so," she replied, gesturing at a tray on the dresser top.

Prepared to be presented with one of her powerhouse breakfasts, I felt gleefully relieved to discover *my* breakfast of choice—Frosted Flakes and cola slush.

"What's the occasion?" I asked, heading for the bathroom and my ablutions, despite the siren's call of all that lovely white sugar and caffeine.

She stood beside the bathroom door and said, "The most exciting news. The best news. I could hardly wait to show you."

I poked my head out the door, my toothbrush jutting from my mouth.

"What is it?"

Jewel wasn't prone to excessive enthusiasms. I'd once heard her describe a four-car pileup as "a little traffic incident."

"Can't tell you," she said, "I have to show you. Get dressed and meet me in the front room."

I showered quickly and fed myself a few mouthfuls of cereal as I carried my breakfast tray back downstairs to the front room.

"Get a load of this," Jewel cried, punching the start button on the VCR.

With my tray balanced on my knees, I waited to see what video would have necessitated my wake-up.

"It's the public television auction show," I moaned. Swigging a freezing draught of slush, I went on. "This couldn't wait until later?"

Jewel faithfully followed a PBS series that traveled across the country highlighting auctions. She always hoped to get a better handle on the value of any products that might come our way.

"No," Jewel answered. "This could not wait. Now crunch quietly and watch."

Sotheby's. The Shangri-la, the Grand Pooh-Bah, of re-sales. The pedigreed distant aunt of every alley scrounger and flea-market fanatic in the world.

"This is it," Jewel said, cranking the volume.

I watched mesmerized. My Frosted Flakes waited un-masticated in my mouth.

"Didn't you—" Jewel began.

"Hush," I told her, struggling to catch every word of description for the item being auctioned.

"I was right. I was right, wasn't I?" Jewel said, plopping against the back of the sofa, clapping her hands.

Putting down my bowl of cereal, I clutched Jewel's hand in mine. Together, we watched the auction with the excitement of grandparents awaiting the birth of the next generation.

There on the screen, was a lithograph. Not just any lithograph. It was the lithograph I had described to Jewel. It was identical to Gertrude's lithograph, the one of the Green Room. According to the announcer, there were only about three hundred commissioned and signed by the Kennedys for Christmas gifts. This little bit of Camelot sold for a whopping $10,000!

"Jewel," I said, squeezing her fingers. "Jewel. Do you know what this means?"

"It means Gertrude Trent's mother wasn't exaggerating," Jewel replied, nodding.

"Yes!" I cried. "And it means that we have a contract to liquidate some of the most unusual and pricey objects that we might ever see. Jewel, this is fabulous."

"Worth getting out of bed for," she said, rising and turning off the television.

"Worth getting out of bed for," I agreed. My head buzzed with ideas. *Sotheby's. I could have them auction*

the more valuable pieces. Get those resource books, today.
Had Gertrude any idea of the value of her belongings?

"Jewel," I said, pacing the room, gesturing grandly, "this is great. You're going to have to help me."

"I'd be happy to help you. But you can handle it," she answered, watching me from her seat on the sofa.

"I know," I cried, hugging myself and plopping beside her. "I can, handle it. Good Buys is going places, I tell you. Settling this estate will bring me the recognition that leads to substantial future contracts."

Suddenly, a very ugly thought tap-danced on my enthusiasm.

"Unless . . ." I began.

"What?"

I turned to Jewel, grimacing. "Unless Gertrude Trent is arrested for murder. That kind of recognition would be lethal."

"Whoa," Jewel replied, whistling.

An urge to take control of my destiny, my fears, and this case spurred me to action. I decided that I wanted to interview Tortelli's agent myself. I knew a thing or two about the publishing world from other artists and I thought I had the right pitch figured out.

After Jewel left, I phoned Gertrude. I told her that we'd meet later and that I wanted to try and get some info out of Richard Lambert on my own. That suited her well since she had some kind of meeting to attend in an hour.

I didn't share with her the autopsy report or Cole's discovery of her security clearance. After all, it couldn't hurt to play some of my cards close to my chest.

Making myself comfortable on the back porch, I studied the newspaper for any hint of Tortelli's murder. Somehow the police had managed to keep the affair under wraps. I figured now that they'd identified him and finished the autopsy it wouldn't be long before the press got wind of it.

Putting the paper aside, I punched in Richard Lambert New York phone number.

"Lambert Productions," a computer voice informed me. "Press one if you know—"

I punched zero without subjecting myself to the rest of the menu.

"Operator," a man with a voice like milk chocolate replied.

"Mr. Lambert, please," I said, in my "I'm bored, busy, and independent" voice.

"I can connect you with one of his associates," the operator suggested.

"That would be fine," I answered.

"Whom may I say is calling?"

I gave him the name of a scout famous for placing movie and overseas rights.

Seconds later, Mr. Lambert took the call himself.

I let him impress me with his current client list and their sundry hot properties, before stating my business.

"I've got an investor who might like to make a feature film out of Kordell's *Billboard*," I said.

"*Billboard?*" A twinge of panic tinctured his response.

I explained that this investor was a longtime fan of Kordell's and that he thought the time was right for a sort of nostalgia piece. Redford might be interested in the lead, I suggested.

Dead silence.

"You *do* still represent Cameron Kordell, don't you?" I asked imperiously.

"Sure. Absolutely. Me and Cameron are real tight. Like brothers."

"Does he have anything new available?" I asked.

"Not exactly," Lambert said.

"What does that mean?"

Lambert sighed and adopted the voice of a disappointed

friend. "The grapevine says that Cameron retired, but to tell the truth, he had a sort of creative breakdown."

"Excuse me?"

"Writers' block. You know, it hits the best of 'em."

Figuring that Lambert still had a possible commission to garner on Kordell's prior work, and knowing that the agent didn't suspect anything was wrong, I let him cry on my shoulder a little about temperamental artists, a tight market, and his last contact with Kordell.

Twenty minutes later, I hung up the telephone.

As I listened to the cherry tree leaves rustle against the screened porch, a slow smile spread across my face. Lambert was guilty, guilty of underestimating and pigeon-holing his clients—not of murder.

After the call, I told Charli, "I think I got us a motive." If I was right, Gertrude had nothing to do with Tortelli's murder. If I was right.

Several hours later, I drove over to Tree Town, Willow Lane, and Gertrude's. I checked my mirrors regularly, attempting to spot the tail Cole said he'd put on me. The officers were either very good or Cole had called them off, deciding that I wasn't worth watching anymore.

Easing the van to an opossum's pace, I surveyed the block. Charli seemed disappointed at our lack of speed. He tipped his head questioningly to the side as I met his gaze.

"The answer is here, Charli," I explained, scanning the sundry homes of Gertrude's neighbors.

Amanda knelt on the sidewalk making a rainbow of herself and the concrete using a bucket of sidewalk chalk. As she glanced up and recognized me, she smiled around her thumb and waved with her pudgy chalk hand. I smiled back. Had her family lived here five years ago?

Across the street from Amanda's, where I'd seen the overall-clad man Monday, an elderly couple tended the yard. An older fellow wearing a fishing cap mowed the lawn, while a lady with a straw hat knelt on a foam cushion to yank weeds from a flower bed. The overall man was absent. I recalled his interest in the younger Connie Baker's arrival, and wondered what the story was there.

One house south, I caught a glimpse of a woman wearing an extra-large denim jumper slipping into her side door, peering furtively over her shoulder.

"Need to check that one out, too," I told the dog, continuing my circuit to the dead end of the street.

Jerry Ritter, Creep for Congress.

One house for sale. I'd call a realtor on that one.

The elderly Bessie. I smiled remembering how her visage had urged me to portraiture.

As I turned and headed back north, I noticed a lot of activity at the Bakers'. Sundry vans, not unlike my own, filled the driveway. They proved different makes and models, but each appeared clean and sported the Maid for You logo in brilliant green and yellow. Either the Bakers were hosting the spring cleaning of all time, or Maid for You and the Bakers went together. I made a mental note to investigate the company.

Seven houses. Seven households. Seven families, not counting Gertrude's place, on Willow Lane. What were the residents trying to hide?

If my hunch was correct, someone on this block murdered Guy Tortelli. The only way I could ascertain who, was to start digging—digging into the past, unearthing their secrets, robbing the inhabitants of their privacy—all in the name of justice.

As I pulled into Gertrude's driveway, I pondered whether anything or anyone could stay buried, buried for good. A body remains in the grave; spirit transcends the coffin. Secrets may appear forgotten, but they fester to be reborn and wreak their vengeance on those who would have killed them.

Willow Lane, a peaceful microcosm of Landview. A

sterling example of the Good Old American Way. A parcel of land representative of all the good and the bad, which linger everywhere people abide.

Paint me, it whispered in my ear.

A portrait in deception, desperation, and homicide.

Chapter Ten

I nearly collided with the back of Gertrude's Mercedes when I made the mistake of attempting to pull into her driveway. My employer was speeding in reverse. Apparently, she'd returned from her meeting and was off to conduct other business.

My horn blared. She jerked to a stop, casting an annoyed glance into her rearview mirror.

I tipped my head out the open window and called, "Who's having a baby?"

She swung out of her car, adjusting her cap, as she strode with her cane to my passenger side. "No one," she replied, shooing Charli out of the front passenger seat.

"Nevertheless," she added, hoisting herself in beside me and slamming the door, "duty calls." She pointed with her cane out to the street. "Drive, Kathryn."

"Yes, ma'am," I answered, smothering a grin. I was growing increasingly curious about this woman's background. The White House Corps? CIA? State Department? She issued orders with the easy assumption of obedience being her due.

"Where are we headed?" I asked, reaching the end of the block.

She offered an address. Worry furrowed her brow. "I've a case. Can't wait. The poor dear might be in real danger if we don't intercede."

Wondering what I'd gotten myself into, I sped across town to a bedraggled neighborhood. These residences were dotted with for sale and rental signs, demonstrating the final stages of suburban decline. The crumbling brick ranches showed the neglect that is sometimes associated with rental property. We pulled up before a particularly shabby specimen, complete with four junked cars on the parkway, two feet of spotty grass, and a frayed roof that threatened collapse.

"Ghastly," Gertrude said, peering at the place. "I don't like judging others by their socioeconomic class. However, in this case, I should have trusted my instincts and never let the adoption go through."

"Adoption?" If Gertrude were some kind of caseworker, planning to intercede in an abusive situation, I had sense enough to believe that we probably should have a police escort.

"Little Bucky," Gertrude said, climbing out of the car. "The poor dear tyke had been abused. These people promised to provide a loving, cooperative environment. And now this." She slammed the door.

I hastened to catch up with her as she picked her way up the buckling concrete sidewalk. From inside the house, I heard a young man holler, "It's her. The caseworker. Ma!"

Gertrude repeated her rap on the window with her cane.

A harried slender blond answered the summons with a baby on her hip. The child peered open-eyedly at us.

"Miss Gertrude," the lady said, faltering on her words. "I . . . this is a surprise."

Gertrude straightened making herself appear even taller and more imposing. "I've come to see Bucky."

"Bucky?"

"Yes, Bucky. When you signed the adoption papers, you agreed to accommodate surprise inspections. There isn't a problem, is there?"

"Problem?" The lady tossed her stringy bangs off her thin brow. "No. I guess not. Come in."

I followed Gertrude into a home that could charitably be described as messy. Toys, mail, and dirty dishes littered the tables and floor.

"He's in his crate," the woman said, leading us into a cramped kitchen dominated by a large metal cage.

Crate? A quick glance behind the bars, had me flooded with relief. A wirehaired terrier, who was missing half an ear flap, cocked his sprightly head at us. A bristly bit of tail performed a frantic greeting as he watched us from inside the crate.

Gertrude was a caseworker, animal variety. I'd forgotten.

"And, why, may I ask, is Bucky in his crate?" Gertrude pinned the woman with a look.

"He went on the living room carpet. I put him up so's he would learn and Jesse could clean up the mess."

Jesse, the lanky teen who had answered the door, sat on a small stool by the crate. He'd stuck his index finger through the mesh. Bucky nuzzled the boy, licking his finger with sweet devotion.

Gertrude pulled up a chair for herself. I leaned against the refrigerator. Meanwhile, four or five other children ranging in age from Jesse to the one on the hip appeared. One of them sniffled openly.

"Bucky was housebroken when he arrived," Gertrude said. Her eyes shifted, taking in the meager room and its nervous occupants. "Generally when a dog regresses it's because of some sort of tension in the household."

The mother shared a questioning look with her eldest son. Tipping her chin a bit, she said, "Kids, go in the front room and finish rollin' papers with Jess. Now."

She relinquished the baby to a prepubescent girl's capable grip and gave Jesse a nod of encouragement as he reluctantly followed his siblings out of the kitchen. The young mother—I could see now that she was young—folded her slender arms over her chest.

"How might you be knowin' that Bucky's been havin'

some accidents?'' the woman asked, demonstrating a core of strength, which was no doubt necessary to survive so much childbirth.

Gertrude's attitude was changing. I could feel it. The self-righteousness that had launched her into this household was transforming itself into caution.

She collected her words carefully. ''Your husband notified us.''

A bit of fire lit the mother's tired eyes, before she stooped and released the dog from the crate.

''Come here, Bucky. Come on, boy,'' she said.

The dog wiggled and lolled its tongue, before catapulting itself into her arms and bucking his head playfully under her chin. With the dog secure in her arms, our hostess finished, ''Dwight doesn't live here anymore. I threw him out.''

Surely Gertrude could see the obvious affection the dog and the woman shared. If there was domestic disturbance behind Bucky's ''regressions,'' I suspected that this young mother had taken some pretty courageous steps to eliminate them. Apparently, Gertrude agreed.

She stood carefully. ''You'll want to use a mixture of straight vinegar and water on the soiled spots. Any ammonia-based cleaner will encourage him to mark the same place again.''

''Vinegar,'' the lady repeated. A stunned relief had her staring at Gertrude as though she had never in her life been faced with understanding. Perhaps she hadn't.

''Ma?'' Jesse appeared in the doorway. A ponderous canvas bag bulging with newspapers hung over his shoulder. ''If we don't get going we won't make delivery on time.'' The boy looked at Bucky, who seemed to draw some meaning from the appearance of the canvas bag.

''The dog usually goes along with the kids on the route,'' the woman said, never breaking eye contact.

"Well, then by all means," Gertrude replied evenly. "He'd best be getting to work."

A boyish grin transformed Jesse's too-serious countenance. He retrieved a cracking leather lead and attached it to the small dog's collar. Bucky skipped and wagged in anticipation of the jaunt.

We trailed into the living room in time to see the entire tribe of children on the front walk. The baby was ensconced in a stroller navigated by his sister. The other kids had charge of wagons bulging with papers, hundreds of afternoon papers. They must have had two or three routes.

As we watched the caravan take off, Charli barked a greeting to little Bucky. The small dog, clearly in the lead, yipped back once. He obviously had work to do and didn't have time to visit.

With the children departing, the mother proceeded to pull out an old Singer sewing machine and a box of piece work. I could see now that much of what I'd assumed was clutter was work in progress and the newspaper mess.

"I try to get a couple things done while they're out," the woman said determinedly.

"Well, then," Gertrude said. "We won't keep you. If you have any further problems with Bucky, please don't hesitate to call." Gertrude handed her a business card. "Or if you need anything else . . ."

"Thanks," the lady replied, holding the phone number in her hand and not looking up. "Bucky is family . . ."

"I can see that," Gertrude answered.

"Family is all we got."

"Good day, Ms. Campbell," Gertrude said, steering me out the door.

I left silently.

As we climbed back in the van, I asked, "Do you figure the husband was trying to get even because she threw him out? Calling the society and all?"

"Possibly. Probably." Gertrude appeared distracted as she glanced back at the worn house. "The scholarship for happiest placement. I think Bucky might be eligible for a scholarship. Just enough to pay for his veterinary care and food."

I ruffled Charli's fur. "I didn't know the society had scholarships."

"They don't," she answered, smiling. "But it's a fine idea, don't you think? I'll see to it personally."

As we drove past the troupe of children, gamely delivering all those newspapers, I hoped Gertrude could arrange a little extra funds. Knowing Gertrude, I figured that she would, without the society or the Campbells being any the wiser.

"There's a lesson for us here, Kathryn," Gertrude said, as we headed back toward Willow Lane. "Appearances can be very deceiving. We'd be wise to retain that knowledge as we delve further into poor Guy's demise."

I didn't answer, instead pondering how this truth affected what I'd already learned.

"Would you like to come home with us for dinner?" I asked. It felt as though it were high time I brought my new friend home to meet "the folks."

"That's not necessary," Gertrude said, as though she sensed pity behind my invitation. Her eyes remained on the road ahead.

"I have some things I'd like to discuss with you about the case," I added.

"I could order in?" Gertrude suggested.

I shook my head, already steering toward my end of town. "Dad makes his special goulash every other Wednesday. Tonight's the night. I don't know if I mentioned to you that my father is a mystery nut. Believe me, it will save me a lot of time if I can brief the two of you together."

"Kathryn," Gertrude replied, sternly, genteelly smoothing the hair from her temples. "At my age I'm not interested in romance. As well-meaning as your matchmaking might be, I feel I must decline."

A laugh burst past my restraint. Sputtering, I assured her that as attractive as she was, I truly had no ulterior romantic agenda for the evening. Besides, Jewel Johnson would be joining us as well.

"Fine, then," Gertrude said. "I accept your gracious invitation. Do we need to phone ahead?"

"Nah. Dad will be thrilled you're coming. So will Jewel. I think her mother knew your mother."

"Did she, now?" Gertrude replied, a twinkle in her voice. "How jolly."

Dad struggled with the rusted mechanism that turned our kitchen table from a snug four-seater, to a slightly off-balance six.

Jewel retrieved a can of WD-40 from her stash in the pantry. Scooting under the table, her posterior obscuring the view, we heard her say, "There, Hymie. Spray a little over there."

Gertrude stood beside me, witnessing the bottom of my father's tennies, which stuck out from beneath the table like two brown-faced rabbits, and the wide side of Jewel's Bermudas.

"There's no need to go to this much trouble," Gertrude said, clearly enjoying the spectacle.

"No . . . problem at all." My father grunted; metal clanked. "It'll only take a jiffy."

I perceived a muttered admonition from Jewel followed by a shifting of position and a quick yank. The table expanded.

Jewel backed out, her face flushed.

"As I was saying," Jewel said, standing and walking toward Gertrude, "it's a pleasure to meet you."

Jewel tucked the WD-40 under her arm to offer a handshake.

"It's a pleasure to meet you, Miss Johnson."

"Call me Jewel."

"Then you must call me Gertrude."

I'd the distinct impression that the two of them were sizing each other up, rather like two heavyweights might before the match.

Dad emerged from beneath the table, to be greeted by Charli's snout in his face.

"Yes, boy. All done." Dad stood, smiling. Gesturing at the table, he went on, "Please, sit. We can talk while we eat."

Talk we did.

First, goulash was sampled, pronounced delicious, and Charli was fed. Then, Jewel and Gertrude got "reacquainted." Yes, Loretta Trent had substituted in Jewel's mother bridge club. And, most embarrassingly, yes, Gertrude remembered having been given the responsibility of entertaining two-year-old Jewel during one such bridge session. Apparently, Jewel was still in diapers and Gertrude recalled vividly her own ineptitude at handling the baby's needs.

"After working at the Pentagon, I found it rather humbling to be rattled by those pins and plastic," Gertrude said.

"The Pentagon?" Dad asked, shifting his goulash to the side. Other appetites must now be assuaged.

Gertrude gave a tolerant inclusive smile. "Yes, I worked for a time with the State Department, the Pentagon . . ."

"And the White House?" Jewel blurted. I suspected she felt excited about authenticating the lithograph.

"And the White House," Gertrude finished.

Jewel beamed. I could see an entrepreneurial glow in the depths of her crooked eyes.

Never one to mince words, Dad said, "Katie told us about your CIA contacts. Did you do intelligence work?

How did you get involved with the government? Were you overseas?''

Gertrude gestured at her coffee cup. Dad hastened to refill it. She settled back against her chair and said, ''I always wanted to work overseas. I left Landview with fifty dollars in my pocket and no prospects and headed for Washington. One thing led to another.''

That was quite an understatement as far as I was concerned. My dreams had taken me no further than Champaign-Urbana for volleyball tournaments and a brief stint in New York, which had left me longing for Chicago.

I decided to provide some direction to the conversation.

''Detective Cole says that you have a security clearance that is so high he's never seen it before,'' I said, stroking Charli's head.

''I doubt if he's run across many of any sort,'' Gertrude answered, peering around the room as though having seen enough of us she'd now dissect our surroundings. ''I didn't know you'd gotten more information from the detective, Kathryn.''

Feeling a tad deceitful, I confessed to my impromptu meeting with Cole the night before.

I must have appeared flustered. Gertrude laid her hand over mine and gave it a pat. ''Kathryn. Independence tempered with healthy caution can be vital. Don't apologize for checking up on me.''

''I—''

Her hand rose. ''You'd be a fool if you hadn't suspected me first. Frankly, I'm surprised you've decided to trust me completely yet.''

''It's definitely out of character for her,'' Dad quipped, going for more coffee.

I glared at his back. I trust people. Sort of.

''You must have so many stories to tell,'' Jewel said dreamily. This from the woman who had spent her entire life in Landview.

"A few."

"It's a warm enough evening," Jewel said. "Why don't we have dessert in the yard?"

Gertrude caught me casting a concerned glance at the porch and the stairs. "That would be fine," she said, struggling to her feet. Her legs steadied themselves. "What sort of flower beds do I see beyond the daffodils?"

Any possibility of our remaining indoors was destroyed by Gertrude's fortuitous interest in my father's beloved dahlia beds, which were nothing but the promise of green and flower at this time of year.

While Dad and Charli, led Gertrude to the yard, Jewel and I made up the outdoor tray for dessert.

Blushing, Jewel said under her breath, "I'd forgotten about the stairs. She seems so healthy when you're sitting and talking to her. You forget about the cane."

"I know," I replied, holding the door open. "I'm sure she prefers it that way."

Over strawberry cream cheese pie, I told the others about the autopsy results and my phone call to Lambert.

"A blow to the back of the head," Dad said, tinkering with the plastic tablecloth. "Murder."

"Not necessarily," Gertrude chided, readjusting herself in the wrought-iron chair. "The death could've occurred accidentally. Locking him up might have been an effort to keep things quiet."

"I think it was murder," I said, easing away from my pie and beginning to pace the patio. Center stage. Time for my soliloquy. The actress in me longed to orchestrate the moment.

Charli began pacing by the south fence. Probably an early appearance by Mr. Toad, our backyard amphibian.

I had everyone's attention. I love that.

"It seems that Guy Tortelli aka Cameron Kordell had a severe case of writers' block," I began. "After spilling out his succession of glitz blockbusters, he'd run out of ideas. I'd venture to think Tortelli sought the privacy and anonymity of Gertrude's home for many reasons.

"According to the agent, the last time that he spoke to his client, Tortelli had called with an idea for new book—a masterpiece, real literature."

"The Return of Sparkle?" Dad offered snidely.

"I don't think so, Dad." I shook my head. "That's what the agent wanted him to write. Lambert told Tortelli that his concept was crazy. Quote: 'I told him, "Guy, your readers will never go for it. You write glitz. They don't want some small-town exposé." ' "

"Small-town exposé?" Jewel piped in.

"Small-town exposé," I confirmed. "After Lambert nixed the proposal, Tortelli told him to drop dead. I think when Tortelli never got back to him, the agent just assumed that one more juicy client had dried up."

"Did you tell him that Tortelli was dead?" Jewel asked, taking another piece of pie. She has such a tender heart and grief always makes her hungry.

"I didn't. He'll find out soon enough. This has got to hit the newspapers one of these days."

Charli began pawing at a loose board in the fence, sending a cascade of dirt behind him.

Dad opened his mouth to scold the dog. I shushed him. My back remained to the fence. Silently mouthing instructions for the conversation to carry on, I slipped over to the side of the porch and inched my way down the fence to Charli's position.

"So," Dad said noisily. "It sounds like we have a motive. Tortelli was going to write a small-town exposé. We're a small town. Someone with something to hide shut him up."

I'd reached the loose board that Charli was sniffing as though he were some asthmatic vacuum cleaner. Peering through a chink in the fence, I came eyeball to eyeball with someone else.

The expletive bit back by the peeper identified her.

Satisfaction yanked in my gut. It was like finding the bread crumb trail. Any time I discovered myself on the right track in an investigation certain things generally occurred. Clues fell into place. Tongues began wagging. And my dear old friend on the force magically made an appearance.

"Phil!" I cried expansively, standing up and peering at her over the fence. "Got a promotion?"

Detective Panozzo adjusted her Panozzo Pizza baseball cap and collected her dignity. "Tommy needed a driver," she said.

"Where's Dot Matrix?" If both she and Tommy had been commandeered to splint up Tommy's not-so-lucrative pizza parlor, I wondered who was watching their "adopted" daughter.

Before she could answer, Dad yelled, "So? Who goes there?"

"Why, it's Detective Panozzo lurking behind fences, peddling pizza," I cried. "You know, the usual."

"Panozzo?" Gertrude chimed in, turning to search for the elusive female member of our force. "Invite her in. I want to meet that Panozzo."

Jewel, ever the hostess, cried, "Perhaps Phil has time for a piece of pie."

Phil rolled her eyes.

"Well?" I asked, batting my eyelashes at her.

Her husband's voice began squawking over the short-wave radio in her Escort. As he demanded her location and ranted about time wasting, she rolled the muscles in her shoulders and said, "I'll be over. Give me a minute."

Chapter Eleven

Detective Phil Panozzo sauntered into my yard with the same easy grace she'd exhibited on the volleyball courts back in high school. She retained the instincts of a setter (the acknowledged "quarterback" of any good team), the power of a spiker, and the dogged nature of a real digger.

I couldn't help wondering what our relationship might have been had I not blocked her perfect spike during the tournament finals our senior year.

"Good evening, Detective," my father said, holding a chair out for her, exhibiting jovial gallantry.

"Evening, Mr. Bogert," she said, removing her cap and sliding into the seat. "Miss Johnson."

Gertrude sat with her hands folded in her lap, cane loose at her side. She reminded me of Charli at point, all stillness, complete concentration.

"So how is your father, Phyllis?" Dad continued as he poured the detective a cup of coffee.

"That new dahlia of his . . ." Jewel snuck in, hoping to keep things friendly.

" 'Phil's Shield'," the detective replied, a hint of a smile sabotaging her stern countenance.

"The gold-and-silver petals were a masterpiece!" Jewel gushed.

"I've got a few hybrids coming along," my father said, uncharacteristically sullen.

"You always do," Phil replied, clever and bright. "The beds look great. Your dahlias are always gorgeous. Sometimes I think the prospect of competing with you at the summer show got Dad through the stroke last winter more than anything else.''

I'd forgotten her father's stroke. I wondered if my father had, too. He appeared less cavalier. "How's Jule?"

Taking a deep draught of black coffee, Phil swallowed and replied, "Better. He can walk pretty well. His speech is back.'' She rolled her eyes, as though we all knew what it meant to have her boisterous old man's speech back.

She cast a glance at Gertrude, then her coffee. "He's different.''

Infirmity had come to visit. Precious health had momentarily tripped away, taking with it our cavalier mood and casual ribbing. Silence hung heavily at the table.

"I don't believe we've met,'' Gertrude said finally. She extended her hand to Phil. "I'm Gertrude Trent.''

"Phil Panozzo,'' the detective replied.

"*Detective* Phil Panozzo,'' Gertrude corrected, basking in reflected glory. "Don't ever miss an opportunity to toot your own horn. You've worked hard for that shield, harder than lesser men I'm sure. Be proud of it.''

Phil leaned back, crossing her legs. She studied Gertrude in the intense fashion she reserved for prime suspects. I could almost hear her cognitive wheels spinning and clicking.

Gertrude appeared delighted. "Marvelous. You have the perfect persona of a skilled investigator. I wish you were on my case.''

"You do?'' Phil arched an eyebrow. "And what case might that be? The murder of Guy Tortelli or the demise of Cameron Kordell?''

I tried not to appear surprised. I hadn't learned from Cole whether the police had confirmed Tortelli's identity yet.

"Why, they're one and the same,'' Gertrude answered, nonplussed, rocking forward, pointing a finger at Phil. "As you well know.''

Gertrude did not know what she was suggesting in having Phil work as the primary. I'd a feeling that if Phil had taken the case, Gertrude might already be needing a lawyer.

"You suspect me," she told Phil, clearly relishing the idea.

The detective didn't answer. She crossed her arms over her chest. A molasses smile finally revealed a bit of teeth.

Phil cast a glance sideways in my direction.

"It's nothing personal," I said, stepping back to the table, tossing a crumpled napkin in the center. "If you cut her, Phil bleeds cynicism."

"Excellent," Gertrude said, as though I'd pronounced her a lottery winner. "It takes all kinds of soldiers to man an army. We've all our abilities and tasks. So," she went on, "what's the police angle on all this?"

Detective Panozzo did more than laugh. She positively guffawed. Finally, she choked out, "You've got more nerve than a barefoot marathon runner. Even if this were my case, which it is not, Kathryn can tell you, I *detest* civilians messing around in police work."

"Now I'm hurt," I said, feigning a pout. "After all we've been through together."

Phil stood to leave.

"Sit, Detective," Gertrude ordered.

In reply to Phil's steely look, Gertrude added, "Please."

Rolling her shoulders beneath her pizza parlor jacket, Phil grudgingly sat again.

"I'm going to tell you what we know about Guy," Gertrude began, "and you're going to listen. It seems that he intended to write a different sort of novel, one that took place in a small town, one that told secrets."

"How do you know this?" Phil replied, narrowing her eyes.

"His agent told us," I said.

"Cole said the agent wouldn't speak to him. Hasn't returned his calls."

I attempted modesty. "He spoke to me."

"I believe," Gertrude said, stamping her cane for emphasis, "that Guy discovered something about one of my neighbors, something juicy enough to propel a best-selling novel."

"And that particular neighbor killed him to keep him quiet and stashed him in your basement," Phil said. "Try this. Guy Tortelli managed to get past a certain retired intelligence officer's security clearance. When this subject of said novel learns the truth, she ices him, and muddies up the investigation, pointing fingers at everyone else."

This time Phil stood for good. "Look, lady, it was your house, your freezer, your guest, and your lock. If somebody else allegedly murdered Guy Tortelli, how did they manage to get the body past you? And if Tortelli was planning to expose somebody's secrets, how would killing him necessarily stop the production of his book? It might have been finished; books have been published . . . after authors die."

"Boy, am I glad ol' King Cole pulled this job," she said, putting her cap back on her head. "Kathryn, you've done it again. Collected yourself another loony friend."

Gertrude harrumphed. Jewel appeared shocked. Dad grinned unabashedly. He likes to think that I at least have better manners than Jule's daughter.

She started across the yard. Charli capered over for a swift goodbye pat. "I'll see you at the opening," Phil shot over her shoulder.

"The opening?" I asked, having followed her to the fence.

"Sure. Didn't they tell you? Convivium's ordered pizza puffs for your appetizers." She stood at the open door of her car all smiles.

My mouth dropped open. Pizza puffs at my perfect aesthetic experience?

Phil made a pretend gun of her thumb and index finger. Pulling the trigger, she said, "Gotcha."

As she sped out of the alley, I drew a deep, down-to-the-belly breath. Returning to the patio, I reminded myself to ask Kareem what arrangements he *had* made for refreshments.

Pizza puffs.

I shuddered.

Either the temperature had cooled off as a late April evening will, or the detective's impromptu visit had chilled our little confab. We made our way back into the house and the comfort of the kitchen table. By tacit agreement, we all seemed inclined to ignore the allegations against Gertrude . . . for the time being.

"Well," Jewel said, preparing a fresh pot of coffee. "I remember having Connie Baker in my home economics class her senior year." She paused, her hand over the filter. Shaking her head, Jewel continued, "If anyone had suggested she'd end up running a housekeeping company like Maid for You, I would've laughed myself silly."

She filled the liner with fresh-ground coffee beans. Always fresh-ground beans.

"Not that she wasn't smart enough to run a business," Jewel continued, "it's just that her hair and the preacher's son, Luke Black, were her primary interests."

"Reverend Black," Dad said, looking up from a pad of paper, which I'm sure he planned to list our subjects on. "Aptly named. A darker personality I've never had the privilege of putting razor to throat."

Gertrude came out of her concentration. "As I recall, in the summer of '73 there were a lot of changes at the Bakers'. I'd come home for Mother's gall bladder surgery and discovered Bob Baker a widower, Connie no longer on the college track, and a new baby in the household."

"That would have been Jenni," Jewel said, fumbling in

the cabinets for some cookies. Sleuthing always made her hungry. Okay, a lot of things made her hungry. "Lovely girl. Spitting image of her sister."

"How did the mother die?" I asked, remembering the girl I'd seen being greeted by the other two Bakers last week.

"Cancer," Gertrude replied.

"Childbirth," Jewel said simultaneously.

We all looked at each other.

"Could have been both," Dad said. I'm not sure he was serious.

"I'll check out the county office building tomorrow for the death certificate," I said. It went without saying that I would examine certain birth records as well.

I went to my backpack and pulled out the map that I'd drawn of the neighborhood. I love visual aids. The others peered over my shoulder at Willow Lane complete with river and the seven homes other than Gertrude's.

"It's a shame to scribble notes on such a pretty picture," Gertrude said.

I *had* done a nice job on the sketch.

She pointed to the houses on her side of the street, starting with the place Amanda lived.

"These people only moved in three years ago. We'd have to go back to the previous owners, which would be tough."

"Why?" I asked.

"They're dead," Gertrude answered, moving on to the next house.

"Dead?" Jewel asked, frowning. "How did they die?"

"Carbon monoxide leak. Dead in their beds—older couple, no kids," Gertrude answered. She peered at the image of the Bakers' house. "I hate to say this, but Guy spent a bit of time with Jenni. I'm sure Connie didn't approve. No doubt Bob would have been more strict with young Jenni than he'd been with Connie.''

Her finger moved to the house across the street opposite Amanda's. ''And I'm sure Beaufort Wilson wasn't pleased about it at all.''

Gertrude had a flair for the dramatic. She waited until she'd secured all of our interest to continue.

''Beaufort lives with his folks and owns a garage on Main Street. He helps Bob Baker maintain the Maid for You fleet when he isn't busy mooning after Jenni.''

Beaufort must have been the overall man.

The rest of the houses didn't take long to dispatch.

Bessie, no last name, was the neighborhood character. Apparently, she wandered around foraging for food with that canvas tote of hers. Gertrude recalled seeing Guy attempt conversation with her a few times. She didn't remember him as being successful at it.

Jerry Ritter. I told the others about my auspicious meeting with this sterling citizen. The way Dad saw it, Ritter probably had more skeletons in his closet than politicians had slush funds. Gertrude seemed delighted at the honor of checking him out.

The empty house on the river had been unsuccessfully rented several times over the last few years. The former owners, having retired to Arkansas, were trying to liquidate the property.

My mysterious lady, the one who lived between Ritter and the Wilsons, was one Marlene Gannon. She seemed the right age to be infatuated by someone like Guy.

''Great Scott,'' Gertrude cried. ''Marlene Gannon!'' Her fist balled on the table. ''Under my nose and I didn't realize it!''

She pointed forcefully at the depiction of the Gannon house.

''If you're looking for a person with something to hide,'' she announced, her face flushed, ''you've found her.''

Chapter Twelve

Gertrude refused to tell us about Marlene Gannon. Instead, she insisted that I drive her home immediately. I couldn't help wondering if I'd misjudged her. Was she guilty? Was I in the hands of a master manipulator?

I took Gertrude home. Watching her slowly ascend the front steps, I felt she seemed weary. It was as though despite enthusiasm, her body bore her soul grudgingly.

Closing my eyes, I dropped my head back against the head rest of the van. Portraits had begun tormenting me. It had started that first day in Gertrude's front room. The desire to render someone's image, convey their essence, on canvas. These would be true portraits, not in the photographic sense, but in a glaring or subtle ability to depict character with color and style with stroke. I saw Gertrude . . . Bessie . . . and strangely, Phil. Phil in her baseball cap, wearing an empty shoulder holster, and Dot Matrix in her arms.

Thinking about the coming exhibition, I could imagine my work of last year—explorations of color and texture, evoking the earthy, compelling combinations inspired by geological phenomena and textile—as a sort of background to this new vision.

"Argh," I groaned. I hadn't finished "The Storm" and here I was running off in yet another creative direction. Gary had always told me that I needed to focus on one type or style of art to succeed commercially.

That pain in my stomach jabbed again, reminding me

that dinner had been hours ago and that all type-A person-alities make perfect ulcer candidates. The pains had been getting worse. As I dreaded hospitals and medical tests, I hadn't had it checked out.

As though my fascination with her visage were some siren's call, I spied a shock of white hair and a stooped beige jacket through the bushes.

Ignoring the subsiding pain, I exited my car and padded silently toward Bessie. I noticed her pause, cock an ear, and continue plodding on. Figuring that she'd heard me, I picked up my pace to meet her on the sidewalk.

Bessie's pink housedress hung several inches below the edge of an oversized gardening jacket. Her thinning hair seemed out of control, as though she'd slept badly, awoke, and sought the refuge of a walk without regard to her ap-pearance. The cloud of hair resembled alabaster flame, the black streak a charred memory.

As I fell into step beside her, she glanced momentarily my way.

" 'Evening, Bessie,'' I said.

She said nothing.

"Nice night for a walk,'' I tried again.

She stopped. Her marvelous eyes scanned the night sky. Then she looked at me. For a moment, I saw blue yesterday in her gaze—velvet dreams, azure hope, and midnight destruction.

"He isn't coming back, is he?'' she asked.

"Who, Bessie?''

She shook her head and began walking again. "No. They never do. Come back.''

Was she talking about Guy Tortelli? Or someone else?

After leaving me ten feet behind, she spoke again. One word.

"What?'' I asked.

"Burdock,'' she repeated, not turning around.

"Burdock?"

"Helps the stomach. Goodbye, Kathryn."

I studied her progress down the block and removed my hand from my stomach. I must have unconsciously placed it there. She must have noticed. She must have figured that I had a problem.

This was a lot of noticing and figuring for a woman who seemed to have one foot in another galaxy. What had Guy Tortelli been trying to talk to her about?

Dad had gone to bed and Jewel returned to her house by the time I got back home. A long drive had failed to clear my mind or induce sleep. When one is settling estates, it's inevitable that secrets emerge, sometimes criminal ones. Nevertheless, I found myself impressed again at how little is known of a person.

After greeting Charli, we headed up the stairs side by side.

I remembered last summer happening upon an enormous uprooted oak near the lakeshore. A ferocious storm had wrenched it away from its moorings. When I'd examined the network of roots, only part of which were visible, I appreciated that the greater portion of the tree lived, breathed, and thrived below ground. Its tentaclelike roots respected no boundaries, buckling the pavement of a neighbor's drive, clogging the water pipes of a house across the street.

Pausing at the doorway of my studio, I studied "The Storm."

As I pondered the colors of this last piece, I continued to feel that something was missing.

My mind drifted to a woman such as Bessie. Who was she, really? What harsh winters and glaring summers had determined her growth? Perhaps irreverent pruning had reshaped her tender psyche. Had some storm torn her loose from her tenuous life? And how far and how deep did her life stretch beneath the lives of those around her?

I could ponder such questions about all the suspects, I thought, dropping my backpack on a chair.

Gazing back at ''The Storm,'' I suddenly knew.

The missing component. In a bolt of inspiration I visualized what ''The Storm'' needed to come to life.

I stripped out of my work clothes and donned a T-shirt, boxers, and my painting smock.

If I was wrong, the changes I was about to render would be tough to repair. I might not have time. *Maybe I should do some preliminary sketches to see what the result might look like,* a tiny voice in my head cautioned.

A jackhammer couldn't have stopped me.

Gray, ebony, charcoal . . . and deep, eternal midnight blue. Yesterday's blue.

My strokes were quick, bold, instinctual. It was as though my arm was not my own, my will abdicated to another, and my vision so painfully true that I must, I *had*, to proceed.

No CD was required to put me in the mood. A tempest roared around me. My only anchor proved my paint, my brush, and the lee shore of my completed painting.

Exhilarated, I rode the wave until I'd answered my heart's call.

I slept in Thursday morning until Charli was reduced to a snout intervention. Something cold, rubbery, and damp nudged me under the chin. Groaning, I turned my back to the wall.

''Go away,'' I said, squeezing my eyes shut against the beckoning light of day.

Cool air smudged my bare shoulders as I felt my sheet being pulled to a point beyond the end of my bed.

''Charli,'' I grumbled, leaning up on my elbow, opening one weary eye.

He looked the picture of animal contentment—head tilted, ears perked, and sporting a look on his freckled face implying, "let's play that you get up." My sheet was clamped in his mouth.

"Let go!" I cried.

He spit out the linen disappointedly.

Guiltily, I said, "Oh, come on." I patted the mattress beside me.

A single bound landed the Brittany full length against me in the bed. He burrowed his head beneath me and wriggled the rest of his body along my side like some canine shiatsu. Not a bad wake-up.

I hugged his rolling, furry form and he stilled, breathing contentedly in my arms. I nodded across the room at my painting.

"It's finished, boy. What do you think?"

Charli's a good critic. Always supportive, he nuzzled my chin, which I took as an affirmative response.

I stared at the changes, which I knew to be the essence of a black oak in the foreground and a woman, worn to a sigh, nearby. The additions were rendered in dark piercing curves. The original blue storm raged magnificently around them, at last having something to rage upon.

"That's the last one," I told the dog. "The final painting in this group. And you know what?" I continued, climbing over him and out of bed. "I know what I want to do next. I feel the concept in my bones."

Striding to the bathroom and my ablutions, I finished, "I am on my way!"

A half an hour later as I sat behind the wheel of my malfunctioning van, I said out loud, "So maybe I'm in for a few glitches."

I'd planned to drive to the county office building and dig up the dirt on the Bakers, maybe swing by a realtor of my acquaintance to check on that Willow Lane house that was up for sale.

"Improvisation," I told Charli, who sat patiently beside me. "In order to achieve temporary equilibrium in a world dominated by entropy, a person must learn to adapt. It's Darwinism in its most basic human application."

The dog groaned. He has a fine vocabulary, but I don't think he likes it much when I wax philosophical.

"Change of plan," I said, in plainer terms. Getting out of the car, I walked back into the house with the dog gamely in tow. "We might as well turn the stumbling blocks into stepping stones."

I swear he rolled his eyes at me. He despises cliché more than philosophy.

As I called for a tow to a local service station, Charli slipped into the kitchen, hoping no doubt for another meal.

The mechanic at the end of the line assured me that, as it was a slow morning, somebody would be over to collect the van within the hour.

After a peaceful bowl of cereal, I was faced with forty-five minutes of free time.

I consider myself a master of procrastination. I can put things off in such creative ways, be so productive, that no one suspects I'm dodging the thing I don't want to do.

With nothing except an empty house and an unaddressed issue, I grudgingly made my way to my bedroom. The former domain of my youth now doubled as a cramped office for the business. My computer dwarfed a kid's sized desk and my file cabinets filled the spaces between the sturdy maple dresser and the "no-hope" chest.

The chest remained my only legacy from my grand-mother. She'd given it to my mother and my mother had willed it to me, her liberated daughter.

"Don't think of it as a place to store pretty things until you find the perfect man to share them with," my mother had said. She placed a slim notebook, which I recognized as hers, in the bottom. "Think of it as a no-hope chest. You'll make your own dreams, my darling. When you've no hope, think of your future as an interest-bearing account. Good fortune, like treasure, building for some unseen purpose. It's a box full of wishes and love. A true hope chest, to sustain you when you've lost all hope."

For a week after she'd died, I had slept inside the hope chest. Nestled in my grandmother's feather comforter, in my own cedar coffin, I'd clung to the lavender fragrance of my mother's honeymoon trousseau. Cedar dreams kept me from losing my mind. In there, in the no-hope chest, I had felt my mother beside me.

After seven days, I climbed out. My father said nothing about my retreat. I said nothing about my mother. It proved many years before her name was passed between us, and by then it seemed too late for questions.

Charli leapt onto the chest to stretch out, while I attacked the paper piles oppressing me from my desk.

Good Buys—invoices, contracts, leads.

Kathryn Bogert, artist—press releases, invitations, hard copies of data bases.

Gary had handled the business end of my art career. This was all new to me. I'd picked up several books on surviving as an artist and the business of art and was trying to learn as I went.

So was Dad.

He kept reading the magazines and books I'd inadvertently leave around.

I spied a list of "suggestions" complete with recommended dates for the tasks to be completed scrawled in Dad's handwriting. Resentment niggled my throat as I picked it up. My father certainly had big ideas and plans for me. What made him think that I had time for making slides? What was wrong with my current presentation package?

Shoving aside my annoyance, deciding I'd give Dad the old "boundary talk" later, I started the computer and set it up to run off addresses from my database.

Instead of art and calligraphy invites, Kareem had convinced me to go with engraved invitations. He had consented to letting the addresses be calligraphied. Pen and ink at the ready, I began laboriously addressing each invitation to the opening.

It was probably my friend Angel's influence, but I found myself blessing each one and telling myself that whoever was supposed to be there would be there.

The fear part of me sing-songed, *You'll be all alone, you'll be all alone.*

Shut up, I told the voice. Nevertheless, I reminded myself that even if no one bought anything, a showing was not a failure. Sometimes optimism is such a hard sell.

The doorbell rang, awakening Charli. He set off barking just as my fingers were beginning to lose all sensation. Perhaps I'd hire someone to help me with the rest of the envelopes, I considered as I went to answer the door.

I'd been expecting an underling to take care of the towing.

Imagine my delight to find myself face to face with an unsuspecting Beaufort Wilson.

I wouldn't even have to wait to get to his service station to start unmasking his deepest secrets and probing his past. *Sometimes I believe myself to be part barracuda,* I thought, licking my lips.

Chapter Thirteen

A fishing shack with hydraulic lifts. Only a chipped sign reading BEAUFORT'S and a preponderance of vehicles wedged on the scant corner lot announced that this was a place for auto repair.

Beaufort Wilson backed the tow truck and my beloved Voyager into a space that seemed tighter than a snare drum.

"Can you get out okay?" he asked.

I glanced at the Corvette three inches away.

"I don't think so."

"Well, come on out on this side," he said amiably.

Firm, strong hands reached over to help me past the radio and gear shifts. He smiled, a nice smile. Beaufort had fine blue eyes behind those large glasses. His wavy thick crop of dark hair could use a trim, but he wasn't nearly the oaf he appeared to be from a distance. His was a simple, guileless face made interesting by a crooked nose and a cleft chin.

"I've got a transmission job on the lift right now, but when they're finished, we can take a look at her." He gestured into an office that had all the appeal of a soup kitchen, its paneling beyond filthy, which was decorated by old Mobil calendars from the 1980s.

I followed him to a gray metal desk beneath two corner windows and sat in a barely upholstered kitchen chair, circa 1950, across from him.

To my surprise, he pulled out a laptop computer and

started asking me basic information. I spied a printer behind him on a tomato crate.

My mouth must have hung open, because he laughed at me. "I could carve your name on a stone tablet if that would make you feel more comfortable."

"I'm sorry," I stumbled over my apology. "That's a new Pentium, isn't it?"

He scratched at his shoulder and picked up a nearby pencil, as though it would offer some security in this fast-paced world.

"A friend of mine dragged me into the nineties last summer. Jenni's a business major and she was convinced it would organize things around here." He shrugged. "I hate to admit that it has."

Jenni? It could only be Jenni Baker. Beaufort had afforded me an opening big enough to drive my Voyager through.

Displaying a trace of coy interest, I asked. "Is Jenni your girlfriend?"

"No," he answered too quickly, blushing up to his ears. "We just grew up together, that's all." He couldn't quite keep regret out of his tone.

Before he could end this embarrassingly personal line of questioning, I leaned closer. "You're lucky that you and Jenni are still friends. I was crazy for the next-door neighbor, but he never gave me a second look."

Business seemed slow. Beaufort glanced around the empty room and said, "Would you like a cup of coffee?"

I beamed at him. "I'd love one."

Between our second and third cup of coffee, Beaufort checked my van, diagnosed the problem, and set a mechanic to fixing it.

Between our third and fourth cup of coffee, I told Beaufort the full fabricated story of my unrequited childhood crush and how the boy had run off with an older woman.

At that point, my new pal's face darkened. Jealousy can transform the sweetest countenances, poison the most gentle dispositions. I listened carefully as he told me about Jenni's close call and how he'd saved her from making a fool of herself with some older man.

When I asked how he'd managed to do this, an unpleasant smile split his face. "I took care of it," he said coldly. Swinging his arms akimbo to take in the shop, he added, "That's what I do. I fix things."

He fixed my van real well, and at a reasonable rate. That new computer of his printed out a detailed receipt, and I'm sure, added me to *their* database.

I have this ghastly vision of the future. I open my front door to find an avalanche of junk mail all targeted at me via the exchange of all these databases. It's almost like having a police record.

Since I was clearly not going to make it to the county office building, I moved again into a different direction.

Beaufort's service station proved a couple of blocks away from Year Two Thousand Real Estate. The brick building housing the office served as testimony to how a careful touch-up can totally destroy the original appeal of an historic building.

Without legal recourse, the Landview Ladies Club had been forced to stand by impotently as the twenty-first Century painted over the nineteenth. Original concrete work was replaced by trendy wood decking and the original tile roof fell victim to a nice green asphalt, which was, of course, designed to complement the yellow brick walls.

The original board of trustees for the First National Bank of Landview were no doubt turning over in their coffers at the sacrilege of their beloved first home.

After parking in the far corner of the lot, I prepared to run the gauntlet past the receptionist and other agents in the building, who generally eagerly awaited walk-ins.

I felt almost disappointed when I stepped inside and discovered myself alone. The receptionist's area was unoccupied although I noticed several red lights indicating telephone lines in service.

Coffee brewed in a new Cusinart near the door. A platter of coconut doughnuts kept it company. The place seemed so quiet, I was reminded of a ghost town. Perhaps everyone was stuck in some metaphysical escrow account awaiting sufficient higher approval to move into their new home.

As I created fanciful scenarios, a cheerful woman, wearing a splashy broomstick skirt, peasant blouse, and graying bun, appeared in the hallway.

"Welcome," she said in a Mexican-accented voice that matched her complexion. "You want to buy a house, yes?"

Before I could state my intention, she chattered on. "We have good houses. Special houses. You like condos? We have condos. You like duplexes? We have duplexes."

She thrust the plate of doughnuts in my face.

"Eat. You're too skinny," she told me. "Now, my daughter, Carlota Lopez, she will help you find the perfect house."

Settling herself behind the receptionist's desk, she grinned up at me, pen poised over some standard form. "You like Carlota to be your agent, yes?"

The woman I'd come to see swept into the room and grabbed me by the hand. Addressing the obviously disappointed Señora Lopez, Sue "Sells" Selton said, "She would *not* like Carlota to be her agent."

As Sue hauled me away, she grumbled, "Big mistake hiring Carlota's mother even as a temp. I swear, if she tries to redirect any more of my clients, I'm going to fire her."

It was a brief walk to Sue's office, a room with a theme—Sue "Sells" Selton—in the form of awards, photographs, and a huge blowup of her signature orange SUE SELLS button.

I'd met Sue last year and since then she'd sent a few

clients my way. I'm sure she figured that I'd reciprocate. The knowledge that I hadn't yet, made me feel a bit awkward about soliciting a favor now.

In her usual manner, Sue hadn't stopped chattering since taking my hand. She recited sales figures for March, her favorite properties, and a litany of woe regarding the future mortgage rates.

"It's so great of you to stop by," Sue gushed, her eager, made-up face still very much that of the cheerleader that she had been. "Candy?"

She offered me an orange sourball wrapped in SUE SELLS cellophane. I shook my head "no."

"I was hoping you might be able to give me some background on a listing," I said.

She peered down her perfect upturned nose at me and grinned. "Is it MLS? We'll find out. What's the address?"

I gave her the address of the house between Bessie's and the Ritters'. Sue clicked efficiently away at her computer keyboard, her blond flip barely moving atop the overly padded shoulders of her realtor's jacket.

"Oh," she said, apparently finding what she wanted. She swung around in her chair, redirected her monitor out of my line of vision, and said meaningfully, "Now, what can I do for you?"

Implication. Payback time. Meaning—what could I offer her?

I pursed my lips. She arched an eyebrow. We never lost eye contact.

Truthfully, despite her exuberance, I'd found that Sue was a good agent: fair, justifiably aggressive, and honest.

I smiled. "Are you familiar with Willow Lane?"

She grinned, toying with an orange plastic SUE SELLS pen. "Tree Town. Where this place is." She nodded at the still-concealed monitor screen.

Straightening in my chair, I said, "I've been hired by Gertrude Trent to liquidate her estate."

No sooner had I gotten Gertrude's address out, than Sue's eyes were glittering with points, percentages, and closing costs. "That's a fabulous property. Has she listed yet? Surely you only want her to have the best. I knew we could do each other good, Kate."

"Kathryn," I corrected.

"Kathryn." She was busily digging in a drawer. Tearing off what I assumed was a standard contract, Sue said, "You will ask her if I can call?" A sly smile sabotaged her perky look.

"Of course." I'd warn Gertrude first.

"Now, what is it that you wanted to know about that house?" A possible commission in her pocket, Sue tipped the monitor screen toward me. "I happen to know the listing agent. The house has quite a history. You've come to the right place."

It took nearly an hour before Sue was finished telling me the lowdown on the house and its various occupants. I had to admit as I left that I'd made a fine bargain. *Wait until I tell the others about that place!*

I stood outside the building for a few minutes, examining the late-morning sky. A dappled gray, it seemed rain was likely. Before I could head for the parking lot, I heard someone scream, "Kathryn! Kathryn Bogert!"

Across the road, four busy lanes away, stood Jewel Johnson. At least, I thought it was Jewel. She wore a black vinyl cape. Aluminum foil pieces were jutting out from her hair as though she were trying to attract radio signals from another planet.

"Kathryn!" She screamed and waved her arms looking like a silver-topped bat.

Shari, the owner of the Ultimate Cut, was trying to haul Jewel back into the shop. I waved, to indicate that I'd come over. The two women disappeared into the hair salon.

What could have possessed Jewel to make such a spectacle of herself? She'd been so embarrassed about the entire hair episode, and there she was, parading down Main Street and screaming at the top of her lungs.

I entered the salon as Shari was unwrapping the front of Jewel's hair.

"Kathryn," Jewel cried as I approached. "You must hear what I've learned."

At that moment, she caught a glimpse of herself in the mirror. With the aluminum foil off, the front of her hair was as white as bleached bones.

"Ahhh!" she screamed.

"It's okay," Shari soothed, popping her gum. "It's not going to look anything like that when I'm done."

"I hope not," Jewel sputtered. "I was better off pink!"

Shari rolled her eyes at me and continued to spray out the bleach from the highlight job. The beautician had a spiky Mohawk in marvelous variations of blond, chestnut, and platinum. She sported an earring stud of each color to match.

Figuring to distract Jewel, I said, "So, what's the big news? What have you learned?"

Jewel's good eye canvassed the room for eavesdroppers. Lowering her voice, she said, "The best place to find out the dirt is the beauty parlor."

"That's right," Shari said proudly, one hand on her voluptuous hip. "If it ain't talked about here, it never happened."

A couple of women sitting near hair dryers, and another beautician rinsing a client's hair at a sink, piped in with, "Yeah! Woo! Woo!"

Shari playfully performed a tolerable bump and grind, singing, "I Heard It Through the Grapevine."

Shari's salon was the female equivalent of Dad's small barbershop. Newfangled nothing, lots of old magazines, and even older customers. Shari had been a teen, shampooing when the original owner was still teasing and bouffanting. Since the place became hers, other than taking on a line of designer hair products to sell at a hefty markup, Shari had left it as it was.

"Okeydokey," Shari said, spinning Jewel away from the mirror. As if that wasn't enough, she added, "Don't look."

"What now?" Jewel asked, clearly out of her league.

"Shampoo corner. It is there that I will further transform these tired tresses into the dream hairdo of your life!" Shari cried enthusiastically.

I followed them across the room to where Jewel was plunked in a reclining chair, her white, pink, and brown hair dangling in the sink like overdone colored fettucini.

There was something in Shari's expression that said "mad scientist" as she pored over a cabinet lined with coloring products. She'd whisper to herself, shake her head, pick up another bottle, discard it. Finally, she grasped her chosen color as though it were a vial of youth serum. In a way, I suppose it was.

"Sienna Sunset," Shari announced grandly, rejoining us.

Jewel cast me a frightened look. I patted her hand reassuringly.

"Relax," Shari said, brusquely shoving Jewel back into the chair. "It'll be over with in ten minutes."

"Will it hurt?"

"No."

"Are you sure I'm not allergic to it?"

"You're not allergic," Shari said, shaking her head and turning on the water to test the temperature.

"I think you're allergic to taking a risk, if you ask me. Honey, by the time I was twenty-two my hair had seen more color changes than Joseph's Technicolor dreamcoat. Now, why don't you just let me work and you can tell Kathryn all about crazy Bessie."

Chapter Fourteen

"Bessie?" I asked. They'd secured my complete attention.

"Bessie," Jewel confirmed from her awkward position. "Earlier a customer—"

"—New one, only been in a few times," Shari interrupted.

"That's right," Jewel said, snatching the story back. "This lady was talking about Landview neighborhoods and she mentioned that they had liked Tree Town when they'd been looking for a house, but when they'd driven through they'd seen some homeless woman wandering around."

Shari gave a horse laugh. "A homeless woman. In Tree Town. Behind the bars on Stateline, maybe."

"Anyway," Jewel continued, "it scared them off and they bought in that new subdivision over on—"

It was my turn to interrupt before Jewel told me everything I didn't want to know about this stranger and her new house. "What about Bessie?" I asked.

"Oh, yes," Jewel said, squinting as Shari worked the coloring vigorously into her hair. "Another customer—"

"—Claire, blue hair job for the last thirty years," Shari exclaimed.

Jewel glared. "This other customer told the whole shop that that was no homeless woman. She was poor Bessie Turner. And then she told us—"

Shari interrupted for the third time. "I don't know how much of what she said was true. Frankly, sometimes I think that the porch light's on, but nobody's home, know what I mean? She once told me that I needed to do a special job on her hair, because her daughter was coming to visit. Daughter's been dead twenty years now.''

Shari turned off the water and wrapped Jewel's hair in a tired green towel.

''She seemed pretty coherent to me,'' Jewel said, fidgeting as some water dripped past the turban to her eyebrow.

''I'll give her that,'' Shari said, ''She seemed pretty sharp today.''

We walked back to Shari's station. Jewel caught a glimpse of her hair and breathed a sigh of relief. No white, no pink, no gray. A nice healthy auburn that held the promise of rich highlights.

''You're going to love it,'' Shari said, leaning over so that her face was beside Jewel's. ''And I don't want to hear another word about that dreadful style you had before. Trust me. You'll look gorgeous.''

Jewel appeared doubtful, but cooperative. ''Oh, Kathryn, if what this lady said is true, Bessie has had a very difficult life.''

I pulled up a stool and while Shari cut and styled Jewel's newly colored locks, Jewel, with a few interruptions from Shari, told me the whole story.

Apparently, Bessie was a Landview old-timer. She and the blue hair had gone to school together way before I was born. It had been rumored that Bessie's mother was some kind of faith healer. Anyway, one day on the playground, the lady telling the story said that she had fallen on a piece of glass and cut herself badly. While most of the children ran for help, eight-year-old Bessie lay her hand over the open wound and the injury closed.

''You're kidding!'' I said.

''No,'' Jewel replied. ''She showed us the scar on her elbow to prove it!''

I'd heard of such things, never witnessed them.

"The sad part was that after that little Bessie was ostracized. The kids were afraid of her and their parents were more afraid of her. So even though she never did anything like that again, she grew up lonely and strange," Jewel said.

Shari snipped away and finished the story. "Eventually, I guess most people forgot about the whole thing. A new man in town met her, married her, and they moved to Tree Town."

"She was married?" I said, not expecting this. Where was her husband?

"Yes," Shari went on. "Had a son, too. A boy. They almost lost him to the polio epidemic, but he pulled through."

"How did this lady know all this?" I asked, suddenly suspicious.

"Her neighbor's husband worked with Bessie's husband at the lock factory," Jewel answered.

"So where's the family?" I asked.

"Gone," Shari said, enjoying delivering the punchline. "He up and left her. Took the boy, too. After that she just got more and more strange. I really don't know how she lives. For a while she did laundry and mending. Now all she does is wander around talking to plants and picking other folk's gardens."

I sat silently. I remembered her cryptic remarks the other day. *"He isn't coming back . . . They never come back . . ."* I saw no motive in Bessie's tale, just a tragic story. To never see her child again—it seemed so awful. Closing my eyes, I tried harder to be objective.

What if Guy Tortelli had wanted to dredge up Bessie's past? Could she have killed him? How could she possibly have hidden the body, tiny bent woman that she was? Someone would have had to have helped her. I dismissed that idea. It sounded as though no one had helped her during her entire life.

Shari had begun styling and blow-drying Jewel's hair. Jewel, at the last, kept her eyes closed.

"There," Shari announced, sweeping the cape off Jewel with a flourish.

Jewel cautiously opened one eye, her face brightened, and she leaned closer to the mirror.

"What did you do?" she asked.

Shari smiled so wide her lipstick cracked. "I softened the color around your face, dyed you a good rich auburn, nothing splashy, and gave you a cut that didn't look like that gray motorcycle-helmet do you've been wearing."

I grinned. "Jewel, it's beautiful." My artist spirit loved the colors, hints of copper and gold.

"Do you think . . ." Jewel began.

"Dad will love it," I assured her.

"Wait till you see it in the sun. You can't appreciate it until you've seen it in the sun," Shari effused. She appeared justifiably proud of herself.

At the same time, we both seemed to notice the tears in Jewel's eyes—the good one and the one that drifted.

"Thank you," she said quietly, at last.

I suspected, in that moment, that Jewel, despite her cheery disposition and scores of friends, had never considered herself beautiful. My heart filled with love for this remarkable lady and gratitude that she would at last see herself as we did—a true beauty inside and out.

Jewel was settling her bill, when Shari said, "So, Kathryn. What exactly do you wear to an artist exhibition?"

My eyes bugged foreword.

"I've never been to one, but I'm sure excited about yours. I'm bringing Bubba even though he doesn't really want to go. I told him, 'It's for Kathryn.' "

"Wear anything you like," I said numbly. Without trying to sound unwelcoming I asked, "How did you know about the show?"

"Oh, honey. Everybody knows about the show. Those postcards your dad made up are all over the place."

"I saw one at the grocery store," the other beautician offered.

"I saw one at the hardware store," her client added.

Shari gestured at a meager bulletin board by the entrance, which was crammed with notices. Sure enough, between *Lost, one boxer named Bruno* and *Lose weight fast. Call this number* was a printed postcard proclaiming, *Support local artist! Kathryn Bogert will exhibit her work at blah, blah, blah . . .*

My stomach flared again. How could he? Here I was sending out engraved, hand-addressed invitations, and Dad had me plastered all over town like some fun fair! His wording implied I was a charity case!

I felt Jewel beside me.

"I'm sure your father meant well," she said. "They're nicely printed."

"Meant well!" Before my voice could rise and my feelings become more dirt for the salon, I said a quick goodbye to Shari and dragged Jewel to the relative seclusion of the public sidewalk.

Gritting my teeth and waving my arms, I cried, "Who asked him to mean well? I can run my career myself. I don't need him going behind my back, sabotaging everything I'm trying to do!"

Jewel didn't reply. She cast a sideways glance at Shari's storefront window.

I followed her gaze. Shari and everyone else in the shop were pressed against the window unabashedly watching us as though we were the daily soap opera. Shari waved cheerfully at me.

Groaning, I sketched a wave and headed for the traffic signal. Jewel struggled to keep up.

"I wanted this to have class," I said, turning. "I wanted a certain ambience. I wanted everything to be perfect this time.'' I impatiently punched the pedestrian signal on the traffic light pole. ''He's made it have all the appeal of buffalo wing night at the lodge or a rummage sale at the temple.''

Jewel placed her hand firmly at my elbow. I turned. For a moment, I was startled by her new fashionable coiffeur, then I recognized the look in her eye.

''A lot of folks in this town like buffalo wing night at the lodge,'' she said carefully.

''That's not what I meant.''

''Would you prefer Shari and Bubba not come? Are you ashamed of your friends?''

No, I protested inside my head. *She's twisting everything I say!*

''And as far as everything being perfect, Kathryn, don't worry—it won't be. Perfect is for sunsets, flowers, and waterfalls. You're not God, Kathryn. I've watched you pursue perfection for years as though it were some sort of brass ring that would finally prove your worth.

''You are perfectly human. Perfectly Kathryn. What you do is good enough, do you hear me?''

The traffic moved on around us. I stared at her, finding a glint of truth in the fiery copper strands of her hair.

Closing my eyes, I imagined my perfect showing. I could see the paintings, the food, the lights . . . I never had filled in the people.

What was the whole thing about if not sharing my art, my vision with the world, which included my world? Suddenly, the whole affair seemed a lot less frightening and a good deal more fun with people like Shari in the picture.

''Well,'' I said at last, ''if we're going to have such a diverse bunch, we'd better come up with a way to get Charli in or he'll really feel left out.''

''You'll think of something,'' Jewel said, slinging her arm around my waist. ''You always do.''

* * *

I decided that I would discuss the postcards with my father later, in the privacy of our home. This wasn't a dismantled answering machine that he'd tinkered with—this was big.

Charli greeted me enthusiastically at the door, white stub of a tail performing its propeller wag. He's a forgiving sort of fellow. Despite disappointment at being left for the morning, he was prepared to move on. Dog relationships can be so clean.

"Hiya, boy," I said, sliding my backpack off near the coat tree. "I have had one interesting morning."

He leapt on a hardback chair to give me easy access to his head inviting a petting. As I stroked his ears, freckled snout, and luxurious ruff, I said, "I've got the scoop on Bessie, and Beaufort, and the Bakers. Sounds like a country-western singing group, doesn't it?"

He nuzzled my cheek, no licking. I like it that way, preferring dog tongues to stay in dog mouths and not on my lips.

Heading for the kitchen and some cold leftover goulash, I said, "The showing is going to be a little different from what I'd planned. This seems to be a day for me to learn to improvise."

The phone ringing preceded our entry into the kitchen. I caught it just before the machine picked up.

"Hello," I said.

"Kathryn," Gary replied. "I'm glad I caught you at home."

That made one of us.

"Listen, I know it's short notice but I've got some tickets for the Lyric Opera Friday and I was wondering if you would join me." Gary had one of those alluring telephone voices. It annoyed me that the sound of it could still play on my nerves so easily.

"Kathryn?" he repeated when I didn't answer.

Not fair. Not fair. Not fair, I told myself. I loved Lyric and could never get or afford tickets.

"Gary," I said at last, opening the fridge and fetching the goulash. "I don't really think it's a good idea. Why start up something that's finished?"

"It wasn't my idea to finish it," he said gently. "I thought that with you getting back on track with your career you might be willing to give us another chance, too."

My fork stuck in the glutinous, cold egg noodles.

Why was I feeling like the bad guy here? Gary had dominated me. He'd tried to run everything. Just like Dad was trying to do now!

Jewel's words came back to haunt me. *"I'm sure he meant well."*

Had Gary meant well, too? Was it his fault that I'd abdicated decision-making to him? Can anyone really run your life for you without your permission?

"I don't know," I said finally. "I'm feeling confused."

"That's okay," Gary said, obviously taking my indecision for a possible "yes." "I don't want to rush you. If you decide to go to the opera with me, just give me a call."

I found myself writing down his cellular phone number.

"If you don't mind," he went on, "I'd really like to attend the showing."

I pictured Gary, Shari, Bubba, the grocery store clerk, Kareem, and Charli in the same room. I was definitely not in charge of the universe.

"Would that be okay?" he asked.

"Sure, Gary," I said, feeling mature and in control.

"See you there," he replied, his voice a caress.

"Goodbye," I answered, slightly breathless.

After he hung up, I looked at the receiver in my hand as though it were an anaconda.

"Arghh!" I slammed the phone down. "Programming can be so deep, Charli," I said, spooning out my lunch into a bowl.

For the first time in years, I allowed myself to remember the good times with Gary. Ice-skating on State Street, sharing hot chestnuts later. His crazy apartment with the faucets on backward and the great beveled-glass doors. Falling asleep in his arms when I'd had the flu so badly that I'd wanted to die.

Sitting at the kitchen table, I couldn't help wondering. Had I been wrong about Gary and me? Was I a perfectionist? Had I let go of a real relationship because it didn't meet my standards—and nothing ever could?

"Life is feeling very complicated lately," I told Charli, who lay at my feet. "My hormones have been in deep freeze so long I think they might be thawing and interfering with my judgment."

He dropped one of his big paws on my thigh and gazed up at me, as if to say, "I trust you. Things are simple. You and I. Together."

I don't believe in reheating leftovers. In my opinion, if it was prepared properly the first time, to heat it again is to overcook it. Better to have it cold and proper. Sort of vichyssoise with beef. When gobs of fat collect at the top of the Tupperware, it does affect my appetite, however.

Just as I was deciding not to finish my goulash, the phone rang again.

My heart did a flip-flop that I had thought I was too old to manage. Gary again?

I answered the phone with a steady hand.

"Ms. Bogert?"

Double flip-flop. If Gary's phone voice was dangerous, Detective Cole's was positively lethal.

"Yes," I replied.

"I think you might want to come down to the station," he said very seriously.

Senses on alert, I realized this was no social call.

"Why? What's going on?"

"Your client, Gertrude Trent, was brought in this morning. She hasn't been formally arrested, but there's still time.''

''What's the charge?''

''Assaulting a police officer.''

Chapter Fifteen

Charli and I made it to the Landview police station in record time. Cole had been circumspect on the phone, but I gathered that he wasn't kidding. Gertrude might be in big trouble.

The last time I'd seen her, she had been going on about Marlene Gannon and handling that situation herself.

Nice job, Gertrude, I thought.

Glancing up with something other than community pride at the solid-face brick of our new police complex, I told myself that I was just visiting. They really weren't planning to dedicate an interview room to me . . . or a cell.

A bored officer at reception told me to wait where I was for Cole. I sat on one of the uncomfortable stone benches. I knew the drill.

After giving me enough time to set my nerves on edge, Cole appeared from the west corridor.

"Ms. Bogert," he said courteously. He indicated with a nod that I was to follow him, which I did.

He didn't speak again until he'd led me into an interview room, which I'd never been in before. Surprise. Maybe it was a conference room. It proved a little larger than the others.

"Have a seat," Cole said, leaning against the edge of the table nonchalantly.

After casting him a suspicious glance, I complied. Charli leapt onto the chair next to me. Cole gave him a look, but said nothing.

"What's going on? Where's Gertrude?" I asked.

A grudging smile did interesting things to his rugged face.

"She's fine. Don't worry. The officer she assaulted may need counseling, but she didn't break anything."

"Break anything?"

"I quote, 'I've never seen an old woman move so quick in my whole life. She did some kind of kung-fu thing with that cane and I hit the dirt.' "

Amusement lightened my concern. "She took out one of your officers?"

"Apparently. And rather neatly, too. I believe he'd have left her where she was rather than have the story get out, but she left him no choice when she refused to leave the Gannon property." Cole rubbed his neck where his shirt collar lay open.

I shook my head. Rolling my eyes toward the ceiling, I said, "I knew it would have something to do with Marlene Gannon."

"Why?"

"Because when we were going over the case, possible motives, she got all excited and said she was going to check something out herself. I figured she meant a quick couple of faxes to some of her former associates."

"Nope," he said, standing and stretching. "Gertrude Trent went on her first field mission in years."

"Field mission?"

As we walked to the part of the station where they were keeping Gertrude, Cole told me the story. Apparently, during the night, Gertrude had made her way into the brush at the back of Gannon's property, complete with camp stool, binoculars, and a thermos of Postum.

"She staked out the Gannon house?" I said, thinking that with her hip it must have taken her a good hour to walk that far.

"Rather well, too. If the Gannon woman hadn't been the nervous, vigilant type, she might not have been caught."

I put my hand on his arm to stop him. Searching his eyes for an answer, I asked, "Why are you telling me all this? The last time we spoke my client was your numero-uno suspect."

"Funny thing that," he answered, crossing his arms. "I decided to pull a few favors myself and see if I could find a chink in her security screen. I called a friend in the Justice Department, who called a friend at State. The message I got back through the grapevine was that Gertrude Trent was cleaner than a new penny.

"Apparently, she's darn near a legend in the intelligence community. I was told that I either got her off the hook quietly or I could expect an invasion of the scariest retired field officers in the country. These agents would do my job for me, and then rearrange my face."

I fought a smile. "Pity. Such a nice face."

"My thinking exactly."

"So where does that leave us?" I asked.

"You are going to convince Gertrude that Marlene Gannon is harmless and to stay off her property. I will convince a certain young officer with a damaged ego not to pursue the resisting arrest charge."

"That might not be too easy," I said as we paused by an interview room.

"I'll help," Cole said, holding the door for me and Charli.

Gertrude looked as though she may have dozed off in her chair. Her mouth hung slightly open. Little whistling noises passed her lips.

What a picture. Her khaki jodhpurs were hitched up her legs, revealing sturdy hiking boots. Her cardigan sweater proved visible beneath a camouflage cape, which matched her hat.

"Gertrude?" I said softly. "Are you asleep?"

"Of course not," she said, straightening stiffly. "Just resting my eyes." She gestured at my backpack. "You got any Ben-Gay in there?"

I slung my bag on the table and searched its health-care section. "Aspercreme, Icy Hot, Tiger Balm . . . no Ben-Gay, sorry."

"I'll take the Tiger Balm. If the good detective would give us a moment, I'd like you to apply some to this blasted hip. Feels like somebody stuck a porcupine dipped in acid where my bones aught to be."

Cole turned around, while I carefully applied the analgesic balm to the area Gertrude indicated. I could feel her flinch beneath my fingertips. Sharp intakes of breath conveyed her pain.

While I worked, Cole said, "Ms. Trent, I've checked out Marlene Gannon's story and your suspicions. She seems to be telling the truth."

"Poppycock," Gertrude replied. "Do you think she'd admit to harboring illegal aliens?"

"That's what you thought she was doing?" I said, closing the container.

"I've seen it before. All the signs were there," Gertrude said, leaning forward onto her cane. "Strange comings and goings. All hours. All different kinds of people."

Cole turned around. "They are all here legally, though I'll grant you she was pretty secretive about it. I checked their papers."

Gertrude dismissed that assertion with a brisk wave. "Papers can be forged."

"They're legitimate." Cole turned to me and explained that Marlene Gannon had entertained strangers from different countries in her home; however, there was nothing illegal about it.

"She belongs to some religion that sends traveling teachers, sort of like missionaries, around the world. After Marlene joined their faith, she opened up her house, since it was so close to Chicago, to some of these people for temporary housing.''

Gertrude seemed to be mulling over this information.

''Most of the time they'd just sleep or rest for a day and then move on,'' Cole said.

''Well, why would she hide something like that?'' I said.

''Apparently, she was afraid that her neighbors might be less than kind if they knew what she was doing. She has a brother, too.''

''Are they some kind of a cult?'' I asked, wondering if perhaps Gertrude's suspicions had been justified.

''They're Baha'is,'' Cole answered.

Gertrude tossed her hands up. ''That fits. I've seen those people get the IRA to have tea with the British. They're no cult.''

Her face appeared suddenly weary, as though all the life had gone out of it.

''It looked suspicious,'' I told her, kneeling by her side.

''I'm just a foolish old woman,'' she said. ''Harassing my neighbors with my grand convoluted notions.''

''Ms. Gannon is not interested in making an issue out of this. There is, however, the small matter of resisting arrest and assaulting an officer.''

Gertrude brightened. ''I did that, didn't I?''

''You certainly did,'' I said. ''And rather impressively, I hear.''

''He was trying to sneak up on me, noisy as a boar in a thicket.'' Gertrude had definitely shaken off her defeatist attitude now.

''I couldn't have done what you did,'' I said admiringly.

''Of course not, Kathryn. But you're still young. Give me a hand up, will you?''

She tolerated Cole and me at her elbows, helping her to a standing position. ''I assume that I'm free to go. That young puppy officer wouldn't want it documented that somebody like me knocked him for a loop. Take me home,

Kathryn. Bed is long overdue. Never was much for night stakeouts.''

"I'll help you to your car," Cole said, retaining a firm hold at her other elbow. He tucked her campstool under his free arm and after a moment's hesitation allowed Charli to carry the Postum thermos by its canvas strap.

Her night's activities and no doubt the long sit in her chair had rendered her legs nearly useless. We took much of her weight as we left the station. Cole took the time to check out first and I wasn't surprised when he offered to accompany us back to Gertrude's place. He probably figured that I would never be able to manage her alone and he was probably right.

We got her to the first-floor bedroom, which she'd moved into following her surgery. She assured us that since they'd fed her at the station, rest was her primary need, not food.

"Horizontal. I must get horizontal," she said.

When I asked if she had aspirin or anything stronger for pain she shook her head and waved off the suggestion. "I learned meditation from some Tibetan monks. Just the thing for managing chronic pain. Now, hand me my eye pillow and leave me be."

Cole watched from the doorway as I eased off her hiking boots and covered her with a light tapestry throw. As I paused for a moment and studied her face, which remained taut with pain, her hooked nose protruding from beneath a Japanese silk eye pillow, my heart filled with admiration for her indomitable spirit.

Impulsively, I leaned over and pressed a kiss against her liver-spotted cheek. A soft smile came and went. Some tension drained out of her jaw.

"Rest now, Gertrude," I said, surprised at my sudden maternal impulses. "You've earned it."

Before I left the room, Nakita bounded onto the bed and

curled on top of Gertrude's head. She seemed to settle further into comfort, and I assumed this was typical of the cat. Thank goodness, Charli never tried that on me.

Cole walked just behind me to the kitchen. I felt his strong male presence at my back like a steady, bracing wind.

As we rummaged through cabinets and located the makings of a light, nourishing supper, we made small talk.

Ever married? . . . might have been once . . . high school? . . . worst years of my life . . .

Evening crept in. As shadows lengthened, we sat at Gertrude's table. Dallying over a bean soup, we made the subtle shift from small talk to level-two intimacy.

My mother died when I was ten . . . cancer, five years ago . . . I've never liked people trying to take care of me . . . can't stand weak women . . .

I noticed that his hairline was receding and that his hands had long, strong fingers with square nails. He had a way of looking at me when I spoke that made me feel as though he could see behind my words.

"Why did you leave Detroit?" I asked, hoping to dispel the unnerving web of intimacy that had manifested.

His craggy face darkened. Unconsciously, he patted his shirt pocket as though he were looking for a cigarette. He came up with one of those coffee stirrers.

"Reasons."

"I read—"

"Don't believe everything you read in the papers."

"They said—"

He reached over and closed his hand over mine. The intensity of his gaze proved as disturbing as the tender pressure of his thumb stroking my wrist.

"I worked vice. You roll in the mud, it's hard not to get dirty."

I carefully drew my hand back.

"Happy you came back to the old hometown?" I asked lightly.

He tossed the coffee stirrer into his empty soup bowl. "Not at first. Too much Detroit in the burbs. Guess I was looking for Mayberry or something."

"Things have changed a lot," I agreed, thinking of the gangs and drugs infiltrating from less-stable communities.

"I've adjusted my expectations," he said, leaning back in his chair. "And I certainly haven't been at a loss for interesting cases. Speaking of which."

"More soup?" I asked, standing.

He grabbed my arm. I looked down. He shook his head.

"Time to collaborate?" I asked hopefully.

"Time to communicate." He gave me one of his serious looks, which somehow no longer intimidated me. "I'm learning to adjust, but I'm not ready to adopt a snitch, even one as pretty as you."

"I love it when you flatter me," I teased.

He rose and stepped into my personal space. He backed me up against the counter one tantalizing step at a time. My dog viewed this intrusion with little concern.

"I told you before," he said, his voice gruff. "I'm not sure that I like you."

His breath fanning my cheek felt as warm as the glow in my belly. This was an extremely virile man. I'm a big woman. It takes something powerful to fluster me.

His eyes seemed gray with mystery, interest, and smoldering emotion. I couldn't recall seeing such perfectly formed full lips on a man before. I must have been staring.

Cole groaned as though abdicating something.

Suddenly, his lips connected with mine, gently, tentatively. I deepened the kiss, enjoying the taste of him, the delicious allure of an unexpected embrace.

I waited for the fireworks.

We opened our eyes at the same time.

Pulling away, I laughed.

"I'm sorry," I said, resting my hands on his firm shoulders. "The brain is willing, the body is lagging."

He wiped his mouth with the back of his hand, smothering a smile. "I understand. It's been a while for me, too."

"Still friends?" I asked.

He winked, turning to clear the table. "For now."

Neither of us wanted Postum so we decided to share a bottle of root beer. Settling ourselves a comfortable distance apart in the living room, we nursed our respective brews.

I communicated. I reiterated my theory that Guy Tortelli had been planning to write an exposé and had been murdered for it. Patiently, I provided the details of my interview with Guy's agent, my suspicions about Beaufort Wilson, and the strange story of Bessie.

"Wait until you hear what I dug up on that house for sale," I said enthusiastically. I hadn't had an opportunity to tell anyone yet about what Sue had shared with me.

"It was rented by drug dealers who are currently doing time," Cole said.

"It was rented by drug—" I began. "How did you know?"

"Kathryn, do you believe the police to be doing nothing except waiting for you to crack this case?"

"I guess not."

"We checked the entire neighborhood for known felons, any one with too many traffic tickets," Cole said, taking a swig of root beer.

"So," I said, leaning forward. "Don't you think a bunch of people trying to hide out in Landview and sell drugs in Pulaski for their gang is a great motive?"

"It's a perfectly lovely motive, Kathryn. Unfortunately, the timing is all wrong. The drug dealers were busted two years ago. At the time of Tortelli's death they hadn't even moved to Landview yet.''

''Okay, well, who rented before them?'' I asked, not wanting to let go of my most promising lead.

''A family whose primary crime seems to have been a propensity for hosting pig roasts for bike gangs. Loud, but legal.''

I scowled. I really thought the druggies looked good on this one.

Brightening, I mentioned our confusion about the Bakers, and how I intended to check out the birth and death certificates.

''Done,'' Cole said nonchalantly. ''Nothing dirty there. Bob Baker and Jennifer Baker are the parents on record of Jenni Baker. Jennifer Baker died the same year of cancer.''

''We wondered . . .''

''Definitely sisters. No skeletons there.''

We discussed Bessie for a few minutes and Amanda's family. Apparently, Beaufort's mother was quite a gossip and had eagerly told Cole everything she knew, suspected, or imagined about all her neighbors.

Mentally ticking off suspects in my head, it seemed to me that the only one we hadn't gotten to at all was Jerry Ritter.

Cole must have come to the same conclusion. ''My money is on Jerry Ritter. He's dirty. I know it. I can smell it.''

''What have you come up with?''

He took a long swig. ''Not enough. Suspicions of kickbacks with construction crews. Possible tax evasion. Maybe a girlfriend on the side.''

''Any one of those things would be enough,'' I said, eagerly leaning forward. ''He wants a career in politics. He couldn't afford to be the star of a Kordell blockbuster.''

Rubbing the frayed edges of the arm of the chair, Cole seemed focused on a point beyond the floor.

"That's what's bothering you, isn't it?" I asked. "He's too obvious."

"Right. Frankly, at this point we've eliminated no one. Everyone has a motive."

Chapter Sixteen

I hadn't seen things from Cole's point of view, which shows just what kind of an amateur I am. The next day, Gertrude appeared much improved. Over breakfast I brought her up-to-date about my evening with Cole, most of it. I left out the kiss.

We decided to take a stroll on her front grounds and leave Charli in the house. The dog had developed a bizarre relationship with Mao. They enjoyed pretending Charli was a mouse. I felt it was demeaning to have the cat stalking him. Charli got a kick out of it.

"I'm sure the detective hasn't told you everything," Gertrude said, as we walked under the bright canopy of the spring leaves. Dew-moistened grass saturated my Reeboks. Gertrude seemed not to notice the bottom of her skirt growing damp.

As we paused beneath a diminutive pear tree, she cast her glance over the neighborhood, looking around as well as she could through the trees. "I wouldn't have been entirely candid, if I were him. However"—she swept her cane to indicate the entire block—"I agree with him. We've eliminated no one."

"Certainly, we've scratched Marlene Gannon off the list," I said, fingering a bud on the tree.

"Poppycock. Her story might be completely true; however." A suspicious glint fired her eye. "What if her

139

brother was in fact devoted and wanted to keep Marlene's affiliation with her new faith a secret?''

I frowned.

Gertrude went on, undeterred by my lack of enthusiasm.

''Beaufort Wilson might have eliminated Guy to protect Jenni and keep her for himself,'' Gertrude said, nodding firmly.

''And,'' I added grudgingly, ''I suppose if fifteen-year-old Jenni and spent enough time with Guy to make Beaufort jealous, then sister Connie and daddy Bob probably weren't too thrilled either.''

''Now you've got it, Kathryn. Peer through the lens of suspicion.''

''Everybody a suspect?'' I asked, recalling Cole's attitude.

''Precisely.''

We wandered to a sturdy wood bench weathered the gray of good years. After sitting, I told her about Ritter. Gertrude agreed that he probably had much to hide. I nodded in the direction of the river.

''Well, the drug dealers in the rental arrived a few years too late,'' I said.

''Yes, but why did the original owners leave the neighborhood to begin with?''

''How about Bessie?'' I countered.

''She'd had her life ruined once by gossip. Perhaps she couldn't stand to have that happen again.''

''I repeat, 'how could that little woman get Tortelli in the deep freeze?' We also need to consider that whoever did this was basically familiar with your house and knew a thing or two about locks.''

I was on a roll now. ''And, furthermore, why would anyone believe that by killing Guy they'd stop the publication of his book?''

Instead of being irritated with my show of temper,

Gertrude appeared thrilled. ''Ah, Kathryn Bogert, you've a keen mind. I'm not at all sure that you've missed a thing.''

I wasn't so distracted by her praise that I missed the flurry of blackbirds startled into flight. The *whack whack whack* of wing against limb came from near the fence closest to the Bakers' house.

Gertrude grew alert, too.

She pinned me with a knowing glance, gesturing for me to sneak across the property with her to investigate. I cast a quick, hopefully neutral, look at her cane and sped off.

Feet pounding, heart racing, I pounded over her uneven yard. Whoever had been watching us would be long gone before Gertrude could have arrived at the fence.

I stumbled on a stone. An indifferent branch tore at my sleeve.

The intruder had few options open for escape—the Bakers' house, backyard, or the driveway leading to the street.

Blessing my Reeboks, I shed my heavy backpack to increase speed.

Thirty feet. Twenty. I detected a rustling of leaves, a muffled curse. Ten feet.

Gaining the fence, I thrust aside some hawthorn. Pain shot up my arm as its needles pierced my hands and arms.

No one. I saw no one. Swiftly, I scaled the fence. My eyes swept the Bakers' property. The distance between myself and the Maid for You fleet. Me and the front door. Me and the backyard. All this proved frustratingly empty.

Pausing barely a second, I ran the length of the driveway. The only other avenue of retreat would be the street. With luck I'd catch someone bolting into a house or discern the license plate number of a car speeding away.

Breathing hard, ignoring windblown droplets of blood speckling my blouse, I reached the fence corner.

No traffic. The street appeared as empty as a movie theater after the final credits rolled.

Across the street, Marlene Gannon turned. She stared

frankly at my sudden arrival and disheveled appearance. Had she really been taking out the trash or was she pretending to do so?

Leaning over, my hands on my knees, I caught my breath.

Someone had been spying on us. I would have heard a car drive away. It had to be someone in one of these houses. Who?

I discovered Gertrude not far from where I'd left her. Leaning against the cracked paper bark of a tired birch, she asked, "Well?"

"I didn't catch them. Nobody drove off though. The only person I saw was that Gannon woman."

Gertrude's eyes lit up.

"She was taking out the trash!"

"Maybe."

I retrieved my backpack and we returned to the house so I could clean my wounds. Bits of blood formed scarlet links down my hands. My blouse appeared splatter-painted with red.

We didn't make it into the washroom, before Charli bolted toward me. He must have smelled blood. This time, Mao trailed behind him.

Making a sound very like a moan, he forced himself into the washroom with me. Rearing up, planting his front paws on the vanity rim, he examined my wounds as I waited for the faucet water to reach a warm temperature.

"Don't wrestle with hawthorns, Charli. They cheat."

He made as though he were going to lick the closest spot.

"That's okay, boy," I assured him. "I've got it."

Dabbing at the blood with a wet washcloth, I revealed minor puncture wounds. "See? Looks worse than it is."

The dog looked skeptical.

"I'm fine," I assured him. "Really."

Sneaking in one quick tongue swipe before leaving,

Charli lumbered out of the bathroom. He'd done his doggie duty. Back to playtime.

Over a cup of Postum—Gertrude's, not mine—we continued the conversation that we'd left off in the yard.

"I suppose if Tortelli hadn't sent the manuscript out," I said, "the killer could have destroyed it and simply hoped to have squelched the project. But Guy could have had the book on a computer or disk."

Gertrude favored me with a slightly pitying glance before dismissing my concerns with a wave. "Guy worked with a typewriter. His storage area proved that he did most of his writing in notebooks and then he typed out a manuscript. Having destroyed Guy's current notebook and the manuscript, the killer could assume that his or her secret was relatively safe."

"Then the killer would believe that no evidence existed to tie him or her to the crime," I said forlornly, pondering the scenario in the yellowed ceramic tile above the sink.

"And they'd be right," Gertrude replied, taking a draught of Postum. Smiling, she went on, "Except that I've found a second notebook filled with character sketches secreted in Guy's room!"

"You have?"

"No," she said proudly. "However, the killer doesn't know that. I wonder what would happen if I let it slip that I had found such a notebook and planned to have Guy's last book ghostwritten and published posthumously." She clapped her hands, positively gleeful.

I pinned her with a fierce look. "You'd force their hand. Be setting yourself up as bait. They might try to retrieve the notebook in a final act of desperation."

She punched the air with her wrinkled fist. "Yes!"

I grabbed her by the shoulders. "No!"

* * *

Gertrude made no pretense of agreeing with me. As I watched her make her way to her bedroom for a "little lay-down," I couldn't help thinking what a risky, harebrained scheme she'd come up with. I recognize such plans easily, as they are my personal specialty. A half a dozen cats tripped alongside her, looking like some feline Secret Service.

While she rested, something told me to go back to the hawthorn. Maybe I had missed something. Perhaps the peeper had returned.

Leaving Charli to his games, I meandered over Gertrude's grounds to the place where I'd thought I'd heard the intruder. This time, I inched past the vicious tree, still feeling the sting of its attentions.

Bob Baker stood scrubbing the exterior of one of the vans. Soapy water meandered in dirty rivulets down the drive. The sound of water pummeling metal seemed brutally cleansing.

Something tugged at the pants leg of my Dockers. I glanced down to discover Amanda—thumb in mouth, hair a bonnet of unruly ringlets.

"Hi," she said, wriggling her free fingers at me.

"Hello to you," I answered. It lightened my heart to converse with someone on the block who was totally innocent.

"Doggie?" she asked, sticking her face up to the chain-link.

"Charli's in the house," I answered.

She reached her sturdy arms up in the air and cried, " 'Manda, see Charli."

I didn't suppose it mattered if I brought her in to visit with the dog. However, I had no wish to pull her over the rusted sharp prongs of the fence or anywhere near that thorned monster. I told her so.

"It's okay," the little girl assured me, grinning. " 'Manda show you."

She skipped up the line of the fence, which separated Gertrude's from the Bakers'. I tailed her from the inside. From this vantage point I could appreciate how far apart the houses were. A quarter-acre stand of oaks gave the impression of a miniforest near the back of their respective lots.

The chain-link did not surround the entire estate. Instead it met the house at a right angle near its rear. Amanda beat me to the gate, which allowed access to the fenced area.

As though she'd done it before, she flipped up the drop closure on the gate, came inside, turned, and secured the gate.

"You're pretty good at that," I said.

She looked a tad frightened. Offering a tenuous smile, she said, "Pretty things. 'Manda show you?"

I laughed. Why not? If she could wait to see Charli, then I could, too. I needed a break from this murder investigation, worrying about my art show, and the uncalled for return of my libido.

"Yes," I answered, offering my hand. " 'Manda show me."

For twenty delightful minutes, I viewed the world through very young eyes. Amanda dragged me to see such treasures as old moth casings and a felled bird's nest woven with ribbon and twig. When she threw her arms around the bumpy surface of a willow as though it were a favorite grandmother, I realized anew what a lovely, natural preserve Gertrude had created. Tough to appreciate when you're doing a commando run.

No wonder Tortelli came here to rest, recoup, and find inspiration.

Amanda was obviously familiar with the property. After a while we returned to the gate and she led me around the back of the house. Shrubs, trees, and utility poles kept the Trent place isolated from the block behind it. I realized that a fast runner could've eluded me in a half a dozen different directions.

As we stood on the buckling stone of a lichen-drenched patio, I stared at an old wrought-iron bench beneath several enormous lilac bushes. I could imagine Guy Tortelli seated there in the shade, creating his characters, spinning his plots.

What a waste. What a dreadful waste of talent.

Amanda tugged at my hand, interrupting my reverie. She led me to the back of the house. Concealed behind a bramble of sumac, she pointed to a set of ancient steps, which led to the cellar.

"See," Amanda said, crouching near the base. She poked a stick into a chink in the concrete at the bottom. A small mouse raced out and scurried into another hole on the opposite side. When I didn't answer, she squinted up at me, guarding the vision in her unpatched eye with her chubby little hand. "See?"

I plunked myself down on the step, pulled her onto my lap, and gave her firm little body a big hug.

"Yes, I do see," I answered. *I see a way that the killer might have secreted the body without being noticed.*

After that I brought Charli outside and showed Amanda how he doesn't play fetch. She did enjoy his attempts to "talk" to her, in a half crouch, ears perked, barking, bounding to another position, another bark. After a while he demonstrated his real forte—chasing squirrels.

He took off after one like a shot.

With Amanda and me behind him, and losing ground by the moment, Charli sped down the Baker driveway, dashed across the street (without looking!), and treed the squirrel in the Ritters' yard. While he paused to stalk the chattering squirrel further, I grabbed his collar.

"Bad doggie," Amanda said.

Charli pulled his mournful face.

" 'Manda go now," she told me. After giving Charli a

pat and my legs a quick squeeze she raced down the block, little legs pumping like pistons.

"Thanks a lot, Charli," I scolded the dog, leading him back to Gertrude's by his choke collar. At this point in our little ritual, Charli is generally totally compliant. His way of sucking up.

As we passed the Bakers' place, I noticed washing was done. A set of legs now protruded from beneath a chassis of a Maid for You van. I realized that I'd never formerly interviewed Bob, Connie, or Jenni Baker. This would never do.

After dumping my dog back behind the security of the chain link, I made my way over to the Bakers' long, slanted driveway.

As I approached, Bob Baker stepped suddenly from behind the hood of the van. I started. The legs under the van obviously didn't belong to him. Baker's face was about as friendly as a bank loan officer's. I tagged on my most guileless smile.

"Good morning," I said, extending my hand. "I'm Kathryn Bogert, owner of Good Buys."

He paused, accepted the handshake, and studied me with a dark gaze.

"Bob Baker," he said at last. He coughed disturbingly and gave a mighty spit into the grass. "What can I do for you?"

I told him the sale of Gertrude's property was being delayed due to "unforeseen circumstances." Innocently, I suggested that when we went ahead with the liquidation of her assets she would probably need to hire a cleaning company to get the house in shape to put it on the market.

Bob withdrew a chaw of tobacco and set to working at it. The way he stared at me gave me the impression that he was neither simple nor believing.

He took his time answering, staring at Gertrude's place as though he saw things that others didn't. With his thumbs hooked on the straps of his overalls, he said, "We're pretty busy right now. Don't know as we have time for such a big job."

I heard a clatter from under the van. Next, a body on a mechanic's dolly came skimming out. The woman tugged a red bandanna off her hair and I found myself facing a smudge-faced Jenni.

Jenni rose swiftly, wiped her hands on a rag, and offered me a much warmer reception.

"Jenni Baker," she said, trailing her hand through her perky hair. "Business manager . . . and part-time mechanic." She laughed, the picture of a young, totally confident woman.

Casting her father a speculative look, she turned her back on him to face me. "I'm sure we have time to help out Ms. Trent. Even if we have to rearrange our schedule. It's the neighborly thing to do, right, Pop?"

Bob Baker glared at his daughter. If a look could lay strap to you in the woodshed, his did.

"I suppose," her father said grudgingly. I noticed that he'd switched tactics. He avoided looking at the house in the same way that one avoids the glance of an interrogator.

Our threesome didn't remain a trio for long. Connie Baker joined us, looking harried and flustered. I suspected that she'd been working and seen the three of us talking. How many conversations had she surreptitiously overheard that way?

"Hello, Kathryn," she said, warily eyeing her father and sister. "What brings you over this morning?"

"Ms. Bogert might like us to do the Trent place, when Gertrude moves," Jenni said enthusiastically.

"Really." An almost imperceptible look passed between Connie and her father. Jenni seemed the only one truly thrilled at the prospect of new business. Interesting.

"Well," Connie said too brightly, "why don't you give us a call when you're ready?"

She took her father firmly by the elbow and led him back toward the house. They had to pause once, for Bob to cough, hack, and spit.

"Emphysema," Jenni offered as though it explained everything.

"Sorry to hear it."

"He quit smoking; now I just wish he'd quit chawing."

Nodding at the car, I said, "You look pretty handy with a wrench."

She laughed, a wonderful laugh like chimes in a south wind.

"Between Dad and my friend Beaufort, I've picked up a thing or two."

"Beaufort Wilson?" I asked.

"Why, yes. Have you met him?" I detected a hint of jealousy? Pride?

I told her about my van problem earlier in the week.

"He's a great mechanic," I said. "Seemed like a real nice guy, too."

Jenni smiled softly and gazed down the block. "He's a very nice guy. There's a lot to be said for a nice guy. My sister always told me, 'Date the gorgeous ones, but marry a nice one.'"

"Sounds like good advice." I wondered how Connie had formulated this philosophy and why she hadn't taken her own advice.

"It's good to meet you . . ." Jenni began.

"Kathryn," I urged.

"Kathryn."

"Good to meet you, Jenni."

As I walked away, I felt someone watching me. It's a sense like a caterpillar creeping across your shoulders. At the end of the drive, I sneaked a look back at the Bakers' and just barely caught Connie and Bob peering at me through a window before a curtain fluttered shut.

* * *

I felt disappointed to discover Dad occupied cutting someone's hair at the shop. I'd hoped to grab him on a slow morning and share my concerns with him.

Through the years some of my fondest memories have been born in Dad's barbershop. Lying on the broad windowsill, sunlight warming my child's body. Studying the clouds through the red lettering on the glass and mesmerizing myself by staring at the ever-spiraling barber pole, my imagination slipping up and down those flowing red slides.

"Hi, Dad," I said, entering the shop. Charli traipsed in after me and lay in his favorite patch of sun on the checkerboard vinyl floor.

"'Morning, Kathryn," he said, studying me in the mirror. "What brings you to my humble establishment?"

Beneath Dad's face in the mirror, I noticed retired Sgt. T. J. Cole scowling at me. Somehow, like his son, Detective Cole, he didn't seem that intimidating anymore. I perceived traces of Cole around his eyes and in the firm set of his jaw.

I strolled around, picking up an old *Field & Stream,* looking at my postcard announcements on the wall.

"Something she's hiding, I think." T. J. peered at me from beneath his bushy, gray eyebrows. "Had the same look about her when she was a girl."

My chin rose defiantly.

"Kids," Dad replied. "If and when they should stop for a little visit, you ask yourself, 'who died?' "

I gifted my father with an expression of tired annoyance. I was in no mood to listen to him play aggrieved parent. I'd been hoping to talk to him about the back access to the cellar and my fears for Gertrude. By the time I had left her, I felt convinced that she intended to go through with her scheme.

Dad looked suddenly serious. "What's on your mind, Katie?"

T. J. shrugged. "Don't mind me. I got no use for gossip."

"It's Gertrude," I exclaimed, plopping into the empty chair beside T. J.

A definite twinkle softened T. J.'s harsh countenance. "On the other hand . . ."

Glancing from T. J. to my father, I remained obdurately silent.

Dad brushed off T. J.'s collar and accepted payment. The retired sergeant plopped a fishing cap over his new crewcut and made for the door.

"Ah," he said, dismissing me with a swipe of his hand, "who needs your amateur info anyway? My son will tell me what I want to know."

With that, he marched off in a huff. I suspected that the father had taught the son only too well. Cole would probably prove more reticent than I.

"Okay, Katie," Dad said, stowing T. J.'s payment in an old cash register. "I see blood in your eye. Tell your father about Gertrude Trent. What's she got up her sleeve?"

I started by telling him about my chat with Cole (sans kiss), the cellar door, and moved on to the pertinent details of the new game called "Everybody's a Suspect."

Dad kicked back in the barber chair beside me and sucked air into his cheeks. After a pause, he exhaled loudly.

"I hate to tell you this, darling," Dad said, "but it occurred to me the other night that you could be barking up the wrong tree."

Turning, I asked, "What do you mean?"

"What if Tortelli's murder was a professional hit? What if he were writing a different kind of exposé and the really bad boys got him?"

I groaned. "This thing just gets bigger and bigger. I sincerely hope you're wrong, because then Gertrude is putting herself in worse danger if she goes ahead with her idea."

Dad unbuttoned the top of his white jacket and crossed

his legs. "Before you tell me about this plan of hers, I've been thinking about some of your other questions. I figure most everyone on the block knew about the Trent cellar. The *Gazette* did a feature story on the place years ago, when Loretta took in boarders."

He ran his hand over the slicked-back strands of his scarce hair. "Now, your lock question. Beaufort Wilson, the mechanic would be handy with locks. Bessie's husband worked at the lock factory and for that matter, Bob Baker did, too, before he retired. Go figure."

"And obviously," I said, "a professional hit man would not find padlocks a challenge."

"Exactly."

That pain in my stomach blossomed into a slow burn. Too many possibilities. It felt like trying to select ice cream at Baskin-Robbins. Talking to Dad wasn't clarifying things, it was making me even more frustrated.

Annoyed, I jumped subjects. "We'll get back to the case in a minute." I hopped out of the chair, stalked to the wall, and gestured at Dad's postcard campaign.

"What is the meaning of this?" I said.

"The cards?" Dad replied, smiling. "Didn't they come out great? I read in that art business book that you're supposed to invite everyone you know and everyone they know to a showing. I even had some Boy Scouts stick them on windshields at the mall."

The vision of Kathryn Bogert postcards pinwheeling across the parking lot, clogging the already polluted Calumet, pushed me over the edge.

"You should have asked me first! I don't need you running my life. I don't need another Gary!"

The animation left his face. I hadn't noticed before how he'd begun aging. "I wasn't trying to run your life. I was trying to make amends."

"Amends?" More twelve-step mumbo jumbo.

Dad swallowed hard. "I wasn't always there for you

when you were a girl. I didn't encourage you in your art as an adult. I was trying to make it up to you, show you how much I believe in your talent, show you how much . . . I love you.''

He hadn't even finished his short speech when I discovered my vision clouded by tears.

''You don't have to be my art consultant,'' I said gently. ''You just have to be my dad.''

''Is that enough? It didn't use to be.''

''No,'' I agreed, stepping closer. ''It didn't. But it is now, Daddy.'' I held my arms out to him. He entered my embrace, hugging me back. ''I do love you, Dad.''

The words felt foreign on my lips. Had it been so long since I'd said them?

''I'm so proud of you, Katie,'' Dad replied, against my shoulder.

I cradled his head. ''I'm proud of you, too, Dad. Really.''

Friday evening proved rough. Not only was I filled with remorse at missing the Lyric with Gary, but I felt guilty about not telling Cole that Gertrude wanted to set herself up as bait.

Determinedly, I finished the last of my calligraphy-addressed invites. With the final envelope in my hand I had to laugh. Who would get the better response, my formal campaign or Dad's shotgun approach?

Walking to the studio/bedroom, I looked at the final eight paintings arranged around the room.

''Ella's Project,'' the first in the series . . . ''The Storm,'' the last . . . ''Blue Sky Monday,'' an airy confection of cloud and sky . . . ''Dahlia Dreamin','' a frenzy of thick layered strokes, like dozens of nearly clay dahlias interposed over one another . . .

The other four: ''Wood: Against the Grain,'' ''Diamond

Web," "Mulch," and "Fur Madness" seemed equally compelling.

In another week, I'd be putting these up for sale.

"Tomorrow," I said to Charli, "I will finally price them. Maybe I'll *consult* with Dad about that."

I'd always allowed Gary to sell my other work for less than I'd have liked. His contention had been that I had to work up to heftier commissions. I had always felt as though I were selling myself short.

These paintings were going to go for between $750 and $1,300. If I didn't sell *any* of them, too bad. At least I wouldn't leave feeling as though I'd given my art away.

Saturday morning, Dad and I went over the prices that I was suggesting for the work. He surprised me by not only agreeing with my prices, but wanting them to be higher still.

"What if no one buys anything?" I complained, my confidence having ebbed during the night.

"So we sell someplace else," he said. "You don't need to worry. That's my job. I come from a long line of professional worriers. It's my art. Let me practice it."

"Okay, Dad," I said, giving him a quick kiss on the cheek. "Just don't give yourself a coronary. I wouldn't want to have to look for another art consultant."

Charli began barking, racing from one end of the house to the other. Nature was either calling loudly, breakfast overdue, or he was participating in an "all-dog alert," a cacophony of dogs warning that our sacred block boundaries had been breached by strangers.

Dad and I looked at each other.

"I fed him," Dad replied, to my unasked question.

"Well, then," I said, "I suppose we'd better see what all the fuss is about."

"Charli," I cried as I made my way down the stairs, "enough!"

He stilled at my feet, satisfied to snarf at the bottom of the front door as if to say, "Let me at 'em. I'll show 'em. This is Charli's place."

Peering out the peephole, I groaned.

"What is it?" Dad asked, reaching my side.

"Your favorite," I said smartly as he took a peek.

The two of us leaned against the door, as though our bodies were barricades to supplement the oak at our backs. We stared into the foyer. Charli barked once.

"Here we go again," I said finally.

"Here we go again," Dad agreed.

Chapter Seventeen

"What's the difference between a reporter and a carp?" Dad asked me.

"I don't know," I answered, wondering how long we could postpone the coming ordeal.

"One is a scum-sucking bottom feeder and the other is a fish."

Before either of us could say another word the phone rang.

"I'll get it," I replied. Several film crews were camped out on the street along with representatives of local radio and newspapers. No doubt this was the first of the persistent phone calls by eager journalists trying to get the inside scoop on their big story.

"Good morning," I said brightly into the phone, determined to remain unflustered.

"You are a real piece of work," Cole replied angrily. "Panozzo warned me that you were a loose cannon, but I didn't believe her."

He gave me no opportunity to defend myself.

"You couldn't let us try to solve this thing quickly and quietly. No. Entrepreneur that you are, you figured that a splash in the press will ultimately increase the price of Gertrude's estate and your commission."

"You think I leaked the story to the press?" I asked, outraged.

"Well, so far we'd done a pretty good job of keeping it low profile. Suddenly this morning it's all over the wire services that Guy Tortelli aka Cameron Kordell was found in an icebox in quiet little Landview.''

I attempted rebuttal.

He stormed over me. ''Or maybe this is about your showing. Do you figure that some of the spotlight will find its way to you?''

''Look!'' I screamed at last. ''I've got as much use for this kind of press coverage as I need a tornado on opening night. I didn't leak the story.''

''I'm disappointed in you, Bogert,'' he said, as though he hadn't heard a word I'd said.

''You'll live,'' I answered. ''Now I really must be going. Interviews to give and all.''

I hung up. Dad stared at me from across the room as though he'd deduced the gist of the conversation.

''Detective Cole?'' he asked.

''Yes,'' I answered. ''He's not feeling friendly toward me anymore.'' My chin puckered in a mock pout.

Echoing my own words, Dad waved for me to follow him into the kitchen. ''You'll live,'' he said.

I suppose I would.

Microphones thrust in your face. Questions tossed at you like rocks. Phone calls more persistent than gnats. Such was the lifestyle of the suspected and interesting.

If Cole and I were on speaking terms, I might have told him that the leak was too calculated, too thorough. Gertrude was behind it, I felt sure of it. With or without my consent, she had proceeded with her plan to catch the villain.

Dad, having learned from bitter experience, granted no interviews. I confined my replies to all queries with ''no comment.'' The police mouthed such public relations pabulum as, ''We are working on several promising leads.''

Gertrude, on the other hand, granted a formal interview daily. I watched her play the press like a cello. They never seemed to get the point that she would only give them enough to hold them over for one day.

I couldn't help wondering if she'd been involved in propaganda campaigns during her illustrious career.

Monday, Gertrude admitted to reporters that Guy Tortelli had been found in her basement freezer.

Tuesday, Gertrude offered some background on how Guy had come and stayed with her over the years. She implied a special relationship.

Wednesday, Gertrude alluded to Guy's enthusiasm for his next book, which was to be like no other, a masterpiece.

Thursday, looking positively beatific, Gertrude announced that she had discovered a second copy of Guy's final notebook, which told all. She pledged to see that the novel was completed and published . . . for Guy.

I stood in the background with Charli, during Thursday's show, wondering just how large a noose she was preparing for herself.

"I have no intention of releasing that notebook until I've found the perfect ghostwriter to do it justice," Gertrude told an eager reporter.

"Wouldn't that be the wife's or the agent's responsibility?" another television journalist asked.

"Ordinarily; however, Guy and I had become very close. He had made me literary executor of his estate." She shrugged, as if this were no bombshell. "I intend to keep the notebook locked in a fireproof chest beneath my very own bed for safekeeping."

Her face shone in mock alarm. Turning to me, a wink.

Facing the cameras, "I guess I shouldn't have said that." And as though she was nothing more than a bumpkin, she stepped forward and spoke directly into the camera. "You all forget I said that, won't you?"

"I'm sure they will," the reporter said facetiously.

As Gertrude wound up the interview, I spied an unlikely couple across the street. With Charli at my heel, I walked to where Detective Cole and Detective Panozzo were examining me with a mixture of disappointment and suppressed anger.

"Honestly, Bogert," Phil said, crossing her arms. "How could you use that poor woman like this?"

"Low, really low," Cole added.

"Use her? Nobody uses Gertrude Trent. This is her party. I couldn't stop her. You're the police, why don't *you* do something?"

"No law against granting an interview," Cole replied, looking at the television van with disgust.

"But you know what she's doing?" I said, waving my arms. "She's baiting the killer. If our theory is correct, he or she will have no choice except to try to retrieve this mythical notebook."

"Mythical?" Phil said, exhibiting a bit of surprise.

"Of course, mythical," I answered. "She made the entire thing up and she went ahead with it despite my objections. I don't know what to do with her anymore."

"Ah, Bogert." Phil laughed. "You sure know how to pick 'em. I guess we better make sure that she doesn't turn up dead, because I doubt if her distant relatives would be too thrilled with you handling the estate."

"We?" I asked.

"Yes, we," Cole answered, shaking his head. "I have a feeling its going to take all three of us to keep up with that lady."

I met Gertrude in the house after all the press had skedaddled, having obviously gotten their sound bite ration for the day. She sat in her magenta wing chair much as she'd done that first day when we had discovered the body.

"What do you suppose happened to Winston?" she asked me in a faraway voice, as she held the one-eyed kitten.

"Winston?"

"My bulldog. Remember, that's how the entire affair commenced. I was showing you where I'd interred Winston. He wasn't under Tortelli, now was he, Moshe?"

I wasn't sure if she was talking to me or the cat; missing her dead dog or making a point.

"Whoever killed poor Guy removed Winston," she said, meeting my gaze at last. "I was just wondering what they did with him, that's all."

I settled myself onto the sofa.

"Your interviews have been positively brilliant," I said, stroking Charli's back. "You've given the killer everything he or she needs. I don't understand you. You are purposefully putting yourself in danger. You could be killed!"

She waved my concern away. Leaning forward, her eyes bright and alert, she replied, "That's fine. I've been packed and ready for that journey for quite some time. Don't you understand, Kathryn? I feel alive. For the first time in years.

"I'll be dead soon enough. Dead for good. Allow me some blessed risk, some real adventure. I've missed it so."

The room proved silent as a tomb. I felt her energy flowing toward me. In that room, which housed the collection of a lifetime that represented a truly spontaneous life, I sensed anew the courage it took for Gertrude to adjust to her aging body and diminished lifestyle. At that moment, I would have given her anything.

"I seem to be learning a lot about risk. Jewel's hair, your master plan . . ."

"Don't sell yourself short, Kathryn," Gertrude said, her fist on the arm of the chair, "Your showing is a risk. You're no coward. My wish for you is that you always follow your path—despite the call of the orthodox, despite the safety of the mundane—go for your destiny, girl. Grab it with both hands and devour it."

Walking to the window, I peered out toward the street. "Looking for something?" Gertrude asked.

I didn't reply.

"The plainclothes police officer that Detective Cole assigned to keep an eye on me is sitting in that cable truck across the street," Gertrude said. "I spotted him first thing this morning."

"Cole's trying to do his job," I said, not knowing why I was defending the man who had written me off so easily.

"That's fine. I just don't want that young puppy bungling anything. Now, tomorrow is your showing. I think we ought to concentrate on your big event."

"You're coming?" I asked.

"Wouldn't miss it for the world," Gertrude answered, grinning. "We'll have to trust that young officer to keep our plan on hold for us until Saturday."

"Our plan?"

"My plan. I was trying to be generous," she said, tipping her nose higher.

"Here," I said, drawing a cellular phone out of my backpack. "I want you to take this. I picked up one for myself and I'll leave it on. Or you can call 911."

"I suppose this means that I won't get to use my little radio transmitter pen," she said, sulking.

"You have one of those?"

"Kathryn, you are too gullible."

"Please," I said, "please, don't hesitate to phone for help."

I left after she gave me her word of honor that she would.

Saturday, the bright beginning of my new professional life, dawned reluctantly. From my bedroom window I saw a light fog brooding over everything.

"Breathing a hundred-percent humidity is like sucking air through a wet washcloth," I mumbled. What if it rained?

I tried to go back to sleep, but I couldn't.

In bed, repeatedly I imagined different scenarios: how my showing would be, who would be there.

Kathryn's Showing, the slasher version: tornado warnings have been issued, Panozzo's pizza puffs, and no one in attendance except my father, Jewel, and Gary.

Take Two: the B version of my nightmare. Cold rain, saginaki, a noisy, nondiscriminating crowd.

Third Time's a Charm: everything "almost" perfect. Ideal weather, unobtrusive refreshments, a respectful, appreciative crowd.

"Focus," I told myself, my arm thrown across my face, blocking the light. "Visualize success."

An hour later, I could no longer put off getting out of bed.

I did a quick cleanup, knowing that later I'd be doing the full beauty treatment: hair wash and blow dry, dressed to the nines.

I discovered my father in my studio. We'd packaged the paintings together yesterday. He was staring at them as though they were time bombs set to explode. Or maybe I was the one staring.

"It looks like you're all set," Dad said with pride.

"What about Charli?" We'd brainstormed ways of getting Charli in past Kareem and I had been completely flummoxed. Dad told me not to worry.

"I've got it covered," he replied, snapping his fingers to call "our dog" over. "Charli will be there, with bells on. A showing without our Charli. I ask you, what's a showing without our Charli?"

The dog stretched like a waking emperor. These petty details were beneath his royal concern.

"What time are we going over to Convivium?" Dad asked.

"Ten o'clock."

"Let's be there at nine-thirty," he suggested.

"Great."

*   *   *

A weary looking Kareem met us at the door of Convivium. His apartment was the entire third floor of the building. His fabulous cocoa complexion looked as though it held an undercoating of gray. His hair had yet to be tamed, and his paisley robe hung askew.

"Kathryn, darling," he said, hauling me inside. "You know how I feel about mornings. Even for you, dear. When I said ten o'clock, I meant ten o'clock. I need my private time to prepare to be human."

"But it's only nine-thirty, Kareem," I said, hoping this mood of his was temporary.

"Yes, darling, but your entourage began arriving at eight."

"My entourage?"

Before he could reply, the distinctive sound of drumming called from inside.

Kareem drew his robe around himself and indicated that Dad should step in. Charli began following.

"Not you," Kareem said, slamming the door in the dog's face. "Enough is enough."

The unmistakable aroma of sweetgrass and burnt sage welcomed us in the foyer. I smothered a grin.

"Honestly, Kathryn, this stuff smells illegal." Kareem sniffed purposefully and stepped into the room, waving his arms to dispel the smoke.

"We are almost finished with the cleansing, Kathryn." A majestic Jamaican woman wearing bib overalls and a turquoise tube top stepped into the room.

"Angel," I said. On another case I'd met the self-proclaimed psychic Angel. She'd predicted we'd be friends. She'd been right. "I didn't know you were coming."

A huge Native American joined us beating a steady tattoo on a drum around the perimeters of the room. When he got to Kareem, he lingered, passing the drum up and down and around the distressed coffeeshop owner.

"Negativity," Angel's boyfriend said sternly.

Kareem shooed him away.

"Your show will be very successful . . ." Angel told me, her melodious accented voice wrapping around me like a stole. "And full of surprises."

"Care to elaborate?"

She shrugged her shoulders. "If things grow clearer, I'll let you know."

"Have you met my father?" I asked, amused. Dad hadn't taken his eyes off the voluptuous woman since she entered the room.

"No, I haven't had that pleasure," Angel replied.

We did the introduction thing.

Kareem announced that he was heading back to his apartment to "rearrange his negativity." Angel and her boyfriend, known as the Bear, helped Dad and I carry in the paintings.

The Bear and Dad saw to the unloading. Angel was very helpful in deciding exactly where to place each piece.

"Ah, Kathryn," she said, as we secured *Dahlia Dreamin'* near a large potted plant, "these are inspired. I am very happy for you."

Always affectionate, she surrounded me with an earthy embrace. "I'll see you tonight," she said, still holding me close.

"Really?" I asked, pulling my head back.

"Really, Kathryn. You will find that many people will come tonight." She closed her eyes suddenly, inhaled sharply, and tightened her fingers around my shoulders. When she opened her eyes, they had the faraway look of appearing to see beyond me.

Worry lines furrowed her brow. "I sense danger. Be careful. Tonight is important in many ways to many people. Take care."

I swallowed the knot in my throat. There was a time I

would have scoffed at such dramatics. No more. I caught Angel's gaze with a questioning look.

She shook her head. "I can tell you nothing else . . . except be careful who you trust—lives may depend on it."

The rest of the day proved so busy that I had little time to concern myself with Angel's intuitions. Jewel arrived at Convivium loaded down with accent pieces, which she wished to decorate the tables and entryways with. A friend of Kareem's, who specialized in nightclub design, decorated the foyer better than I had dreamed.

Twinkling Italian lights hung recklessly over painted white branches hung from the ceiling. Swashes of fluid material wound throughout. It was a delightful mood setter— fanciful, elegant, and warming. In certain corners, lights wound discreetly up mock ficus. And everywhere there were flowers. Kareem seemed delighted to fuss over huge vases of ivory lilies and ostrich ferns. For accents on the tables, he floated white orchids. Sprigs of lily of the valley lay carelessly here and there. Everything seemed designed to enhance, not distract from, the paintings.

It proved nearly three o'clock before we were finished. The hors d'oeuvres had been delivered: shrimp cocktail, miniature spinach quiche, Hawaiian meatballs, plus assorted cheeses and crackers. No pizza puffs.

As I prepared to leave, Kareem called loudly from the foyer, "Kathryn, darling. More of your *friends* have arrived."

Casting a quick glance at Dad, I hustled off to the front of the coffeehouse. The way he had said "friend" seemed almost a snarl.

Waiting beside Kareem, with her hundred-kilowatt smile, sleek leopard pants and clingy black tank top, was the local disc jockey and a former client, Frolic Galbreath. Her husband Bruce, not one of my favorite people, stood reluctantly beside her.

"They claim that they're here to set up the Muzak," Kareem said.

Bruce bristled. "See," he said to Frolic, "I told you she didn't want you here. If she'd wanted us, she would have called."

Frolic appeared confused as she peered around the elegant surroundings and noticed the less-than-enthusiastic expression on my face.

Before the animation dimmed completely in her eyes, I said, "Don't be ridiculous, Bruce. This is a lovely surprise."

Kareem made as though he were going to protest and I turned my back to him. With my arm through Frolic's we strolled through Convivium.

"I didn't call you because I know what a tight schedule you have," I fibbed with my fingers crossed.

Frolic examined the intimate rooms and cast a nervous glance at Bruce, who seemed his usual smug self. "I'm not sure, Kathryn. I don't want to do anything that's going to break the mood."

"You won't," I assured her.

I'd taken us to the French doors, which led to the stone patio. A red-and-white canopy had been set up to accommodate a bar, and small groupings of chairs were arranged around the perimeter of a fern garden.

"If you think this will work," I said, deferring to their opinion, "I think it would be great if you could set up out here."

"Oh, yeah," Frolic said, tossing her waist-length rippling tresses over her shoulder. "We can put my light bars over here. My table right there. This space will make a great dance floor."

Kareem grabbed me by the elbow and yanked me to the side. "Are you trying to turn this into *Saturday Night Fever*? More than *your* reputation is at stake here."

"It will be fine," I assured him. "She'll play swing and jazz. Some of the old favorites. It'll be perfect."

"Perfect," he grumbled. "First ceremonies, and now this. I hope you have no further surprises up your lovely creative sleeves."

I assured him that I hadn't. Then, guiltily I remembered Charli and wondered what my father had cooked up.

My dog had spent the day sunning himself in the yard at Convivium, greeting passerbys, and intimidating squirrels. He seemed ready to leave when we'd finished with Frolic and Bruce.

"Do you really think the disc jockey thing is a good idea?" Dad asked.

"I wouldn't have planned it that way, but what could I do? Make her feel like she wasn't good enough, like she wasn't welcome?"

"You could have," Dad said carefully. "In the past, you might have."

I paused and scanned Main Street; the hodgepodge of spruced up old, blaringly new, and hopelessly suburban buildings. The city's spiffy new planters awaiting annual plantings, the bright flags rippling in the breeze from light poles, boasting anniversaries of churches, schools, and fraternal organizations. It wasn't State Street, but it was a great street.

"But I didn't," I replied contentedly. "Come on, Charli. Time to head home."

The dog capered over. We climbed into my van to move on to Phase Two of Kathryn's Big Day.

Jewel forced me to eat a light supper. I swore I couldn't eat a thing. I was sure I'd never keep it down.

"You need food regularly like a race horse, Kathryn. Eat," she told me.

Surprisingly I finished every drop of lemon rice soup and a buttermilk biscuit.

In the shower, I exfoliated my skin, I shaved, I washed and conditioned my hair, I dallied under the water wondering how I could have gotten myself into such a vulnerable position again—showing my work.

After finally emerging from the shower, I blew-dry my hair, my impossible reckless, wavy blond hair. Jewel must have heard the grunting and groaning from the hallway.

"Kathryn," she called. "Leave your hair alone. You're just working up a sweat and you'll need another shower."

"It's awful," I cried.

"I'm sure it's not. At least it's not pink. Now come out here and look at your dress."

Jewel had convinced me to allow her to design me a dress for the showing. I had told her that my wardrobe was filled with interesting garments, but she had persevered. Now, I could hear the eagerness in her voice as she waited to present me with my special gift.

Tugging my terry-cloth robe around me, I emerged from the steam-filled bathroom. Before Jewel could say anything, I glanced down at Charli, who was seated at her feet.

"What are you wearing?!" I asked, in mock horror.

He tipped his head, possibly insulted. The neat derby someone had affixed between his ears with an elastic string tipped like the tower of Pisa. If the derby wasn't enough, someone had attached to his dress collar a modified tuxedo bib and black tie. If Fred Astaire had been a Brittany, they might have been twins.

"He's going formal tonight," Dad said, sticking his head out of his bedroom. "I think he looks like a real mensch."

"You look wonderful, Charli," I told the dog. Dad had obviously had more success washing and blow drying the dog than I'd had on myself. Charli's withers flowed pure white, his ears were fluffy perfection. "Now, how is he going to get in?" I called to Dad.

"Got it covered, Katie," he yelled back, retreating into his room. "Don't give it another thought."

"Come on, Kathryn," Jewel called from my room, obviously eager for me to see her handiwork.

"Oh," I cried when I spied the garment she held before her. "Jewel, it's gorgeous."

My fingers itched to stroke the glittering midnight blue draped bodice, the mid-calf scalloped hemline.

"It's perfect." I held it against me and looked in the mirror. "Elegant. I love the color."

Jewel's face shone with joy. "Well, let's try her on, shall we?"

The silken material fit like a glove, cinched at the waist, the back scooped intriguingly low with the same draped effect as the bodice in the front.

"Here," Jewel said, drawing a velvet box from her purse. "These were my mother's. I thought they might go."

I opened the box and found a sapphire cluster of earrings and a matching choker winking at me. Real or not, I loved the look.

"And here are your shoes, Cinderella," Jewel said.

I slipped on the Italian silk sandals dyed to match the dress. Politically, I never hobble myself to fashion. Just this once, Jewel convinced me to show my long legs to their advantage.

Having never gone to prom or any other high school dances, this was what I imagined I might have missed. Had my mother been alive, perhaps she and I would have enacted a similar ritual. I gave Jewel a hug.

When I finally looked in the full mirror, my smile froze on my face. My hair really was a nightmare.

"Oh, Katie," my father said, resplendent in the doorway wearing a rented tux. "You are a vision."

"Thanks," I replied with forced enthusiasm.

I saw Dad and Jewel share a look. She pointed to her head. Dad nodded.

"These came for you earlier," he said, passing me a corsage box.

"Really?" I opened it up. Inside lay a hair piece of ivory roses, seed pearls, and baby's breath. A bit of sapphire webbing formed a button effect.

I took me a moment to notice the card.

I remember how beautiful your hair looked adorned with flowers. Break a leg, babe. Gary.

Looking up at my father, he offered an apologetic shrug. "He phoned and asked what you were wearing. When he explained why he wanted to know, I didn't think you'd mind."

Dad had always had a soft spot for Gary.

"Let me help you," Jewel offered. Within minutes, with a lot of pins and the hair piece, my hair was transformed into something magical to match the sparkle in the dress.

"I guess that's it," I said, hardly believing the woman in the mirror was me. "I'll meet you at Convivium later."

As I slung my black backpack over my shoulder, I heard the two of them start laughing hysterically.

What?

I don't go anywhere without my trusty backpack.

On my way to the coffeehouse, I phoned Gertrude with my new cellular phone. She took her time answering.

"What took you so long?" I asked, trying to steer and talk at the same time. New experience.

"I'm not used to this newfangled thing," Gertrude snapped.

"You're still coming, right?"

"Certainly, got my bells on. Detective Cole replaced the plainclothesman with a squad car and a uniformed officer." She paused, as though she might be looking out a window.

"I think it might be that fellow I tangled with at Marlene's." She laughed heartily.

"Good. Now I want you to wait for Detective Panozzo. She'll escort you to the showing."

"Is this really necessary?" Gertrude asked tiredly.

"Yes. You're the one who set up this little trap. There's no way any of us are leaving you alone in that house. Tonight's a perfect night for 'whoever' to make an attempt."

"Of course, you're right, dear," Gertrude replied, suddenly compliant. "Kathryn, I'm sure tonight will be a triumph."

"Thank you," I said, pulling into the Convivium parking lot. "I'll see you later."

"Good night, Kathryn."

Turning off the phone and stuffing it in my backpack, I shook my head. Gertrude Trent was something else. Thank goodness, she'd consented to come to the showing with Phil. I don't think I would have been able to focus on tonight at all if I had had to worry about her.

Kareem met me at the door, his sour mood long gone. An air kiss for my cheek. "Lose the backpack, darling, and you'll look fabulous."

I let him stow it in a nearby cabinet.

"Kareem," I said appreciatively as I wandered from room to room. "This is *fabulous*."

The coffeehouse's recessed lighting proved ideal for showcasing my work. It was as though the entire building had been constructed specifically to enhance my art. My personal Guggenheim.

Strains of Tommy Dorsey floated in from the patio.

"Your friends cleaned up nicely for the gig. They just might work out," Kareem said, offering a crooked smile.

Each room held a plethora of exotic delicate aromas—a trace of sweetgrass, lilies, and fresh ground Kona coffee beans. It was a feast for the senses.

Together, Kareem and I checked the wall clock.

We were scheduled to open at 7:00. Now all we needed were the people.

My palms began sweating by 6:50 when no one had arrived. Five minutes later, I felt marginally relieved to welcome Dad and Jewel. I noticed Kareem literally biting his nails in the hallway.

What if no one came? I would never exhibit again. Never.

Just as the silence in the coffeehouse proved almost deafening, even Frolic had somehow let "dead air" creep in, cars began pulling into the lot.

Jewel and Dad positioned themselves near the doorway to offer a guest registry. (Dad hoped to augment our data base.) Kareem played the host, bringing people of note and not of note to meet me.

"This is . . ." Kareem faltered, looking at wild-haired Shari in a red sequined cocktail dress and Bubba in a crushed red velvet tux.

"Oh, we know each other," Shari interrupted. She gave me a quick hug and then did something subtle to my hair. "Let's go, Bubba, we want to look at all of Kathryn's pretty pictures."

As she tugged him away, Kareem mouthed, "pretty pictures?"

For the next forty-five minutes a steady stream of friends and strangers came through. My face began aching. I'd lost count of how many times puzzled guests had pointed to my paintings and asked, "What does it mean?"

"Kathryn," Kareem called, puffed like a peacock. "I'd like to introduce Hal Goldstein of the Goldstein Gallery on Michigan Avenue."

"Mr. Goldstein," I said, shaking his hand, trying not to appear shocked. "Thank you so much for coming." I didn't recall him on my list of invites.

His next words explained his presence.

"Yes, well. My wife's cousin's brother asked me if I could stop by . . . I'm not sure I see him . . ."

Kareem and I gazed around the room. I guessed the distant relative to be the distinguished looking man studying "The Storm." Sure enough, Goldstein waved in that direction.

My teeth nearly fell out when Bubba hustled across the room and enveloped Goldstein in a bear hug. "Glad you could make it, Hal. You know I don't know diddly-squat about art, but I thought you might do Kathryn some good."

For a moment, I thought Kareem might drop to the floor and kiss Bubba's feet. Either that, or pass out entirely.

"Quite a coup," a familiar voice said near my ear. "The Goldstein Gallery."

I turned with a smile to welcome Gary. "Isn't it great?" I said, nearly giddy with happiness. "Everyone seems to really be enjoying themselves."

"Yes, they are," Gary agreed. "The paintings . . . I've never seen anything like them. And you, you look stunning."

"Thanks for the flowers," I said, reaching up to touch a rose.

I was saved from further intimacies with my guest by Buffy Ballantine. She'd surprised me by showing up with her estranged husband Sterling. They made quite a pair. Her in her fancy Western garb and mushmouth and him staid in his corporate perfect self.

"Kathryn," Buffy said, "I declare your paintin's are just so fine, aren't they, Sterlin'?"

By way of an answer Sterling nodded and said, "Kathryn."

"Sterlin' and I have just bought 'Mulch.' I told him it reminds me of the mess we'd made of our lives," Buffy said, reaching up and patting Sterling's cheek good-naturedly.

"Rather surrealistic," Sterling said, nonplussed.

My father pulled me to the side.

"Katie, Katie. You've already sold five paintings!"

"You're kidding!"

"When it comes to money, I don't kid."

"Dad, that's great." It took a lot of self-control not to jump up and down in those Italian sandals.

Suddenly a commotion at the door drew my attention.

"I'm sorry, sir," I heard Kareem's voice carry over the crowd. "But you can't bring that dog in here."

I hustled through the patrons to discover—standing in the doorway—my dog. Our dog, Charli. Charli in a tuxedo and harness. Holding onto the harness was the mysterious Oracle from the Video Box. Wearing his monk's sweatshirt and dark glasses, the Oracle told Kareem, "That's not just a dog as you can see. He's guiding me so let him be."

The Oracle was a video trivia genius who spoke in terrible rhyme.

Charli looked marvelous. The halter did not deter from his tux and derby one bit. He wagged his tail at me. Dad looked smug.

Kareem stepped closer to the not diminutive Oracle and hissed, "If you can't see, what are you doing at an art showing?"

"Oh, simple man, who art truly blind,

I know you're ignorant and I don't mind.

I've come to support my friend tonight,

so get out of my way, or prepare to fight."

He delivered the final words with just enough real menace to make Kareem give way. Charli led the Oracle to me. I greeted them both.

"I can't believe you did this," I told the Oracle.

"I'll play the part. I dig art."

I'd been so busy that I hadn't had a chance to wonder about Gertrude much at all. Consequently, I was relieved to see Phil, uncharacteristically garbed in a silk tunic and pants, speaking to Cole across the room.

I swept over, feeling like queen for the day.

"Where's Gertrude?" I asked.

Phil, instantly suspicious, said, "She's not here?

"You were supposed to pick her up!" I cried.

"I know that," Phil gritted out. "Tommy was late and I had to take care of Dot Matrix before I could change and leave. By the time I got to Gertrude's there was a note on her door saying that she'd come by taxi."

Cole and I moved swiftly to a more discrete corner of the coffeehouse. Phil followed. While Cole had himself patched into the uniformed officer guarding Gertrude's house, I phoned her on the cellular phone. I had a bad feeling about this.

We hung up simultaneously.

"The officer says the house is dark. He didn't see anyone leave."

"Darn," Phil muttered.

"She's not answering her phone either," I said, fear and guilt running a close race.

Chapter Eighteen

I found Kareem quickly. "I have to go," I told him.

"Go? You can't go. This is your showing!"

Charli must have sensed something. From across the room, I saw him straining at his harness.

"Lives are at stake." I gave Kareem a quick kiss. "Thanks for everything. Hold down the fort."

Grabbing my backpack, I raced out. Charli must have broken loose. He was right behind me. We were just in time to catch Phil and Cole getting into his Mustang.

I leapt into the backseat. Charli plunged after me, his harness bobbing in my face.

"Where do you think you're going?" Phil said, checking her service revolver, which had been in her purse.

"With you," I said, shucking my heels and pulling a pair of Reeboks out of my backpack.

"Just go," Phil told Cole. "We don't have time to argue with her."

Cole raced lights no siren over to Tree Town. I tugged off Charli's harness and derby. The tuxedo seemed stuck to his dress collar.

"You figure that she's trying to catch the murderer herself?" Cole said.

"She may have fallen and gotten hurt," Phil offered.

"She could have overslept," I suggested, forgetting the note on the door.

We were all silent.

"She's trying to pull this thing off by herself," Cole said grimly.

"I can't believe I didn't see through her act," I said in frustration.

"She's good," Phil said. "She's really good."

As we neared the house, Cole explained its layout to Phil, I told them both of the back entrance I'd discovered.

The uniform cop seemed alert and eager when we arrived. It was the guy Gertrude had popped.

"I've detected no movement in the house, sir," he told Cole.

"You keep an eye on the front of the place. Don't let anyone leave, but don't kill one of us," Cole added.

"I'll take the front," Phil said, her revolver at the ready.

"I'll show you the back," I told Cole.

"Stay here. I'll find it myself."

Charli and I did as he'd ordered for a full two seconds before tearing off after him. He nearly shot me when I jumped up behind him at the cellar stairs. Pulling a sturdy flathead screwdriver from my backpack and handing it to him, I said, "You might need this."

"Control that dog," he grumbled as he forced the door ajar.

"Absolutely," I assured him, wishing I'd left the harness on.

The cellar proved creepier at night than it had ever been during the day. Our flashlights played eerily against the grated storage areas. Nevertheless, we made good time up to the main floor. It seemed every corner held a pair of glowing cat eyes, which were either condemning us or urging us forward. Charli hung tightly at my heel.

My heart felt as though it were pounding in my throat. That little voice, the one in my mind that I routinely ignore, screamed, *Danger! Danger!*

The house proved so quiet that I didn't know what I feared more, encountering a killer or discovering that Gertrude might possibly have died of natural causes. Charli's nails clicked against the wood floor. Cole gave him a disgusted look. I swear the dog lightened his step, nearly tiptoeing.

We encountered no one on our way to Gertrude's bedroom. Every room, every hall proved chillingly empty.

Phil arrived at one side of Gertrude's bedroom door as Cole and I pressed against the wall on the other. I clung to Charli's collar, willing him to obedience.

From inside the room a faint glow pooled on the floor at our feet. I had the impression of candlelight. Voices carried. One man. One woman.

"You don't want to do this," I heard Gertrude say.

Charli tugged. I pulled him to stillness.

"You've given me no choice," the man replied. I couldn't identify his low voice. The gritty determination in it had my mouth going dry.

"But if it was an accident," Gertrude said, "the authorities will understand. If you kill me, you'll simply perpetuate the lies. You'll never be at peace. Never."

What were Phil and Cole waiting for? The guy could have a gun or a knife or . . . I don't know! I considered letting Charli free. Somebody had to do something.

"But the secrets will die with you," the man answered severely. "Give me the notebook."

"Come here and get it," she said slyly.

The three of us looked at one another. She was going to do something reckless. Phil and Cole burst into the open doorway, guns drawn.

"Police! Don't move."

I flipped the overhead light switch. Charli bounded across the room.

Gertrude stood gamely near the wall, her cane raised menacingly in her fist. Charli planted himself at her feet, snarling at the assailant. A man held a tire iron poised above his head.

The overhead light pinned Bob Baker in the middle of the room. For a moment, desperation contorted his features. Charli would never let him reach Gertrude, I assured myself.

His glance shot to the window. He made a single lunge for freedom.

"Don't do it," Cole told him, his voice cold and unyielding.

Baker froze. As though he'd finally comprehended the futility of his predicament, his rage fled. He looked tall and strong, but utterly defeated.

"Drop it," Phil ordered. The tire iron slid from Baker's hand to the floor.

As Phil began cuffing Baker, Cole read him his rights.

"Gertrude!" I cried, striding across the room. "I don't know whether to hug you or kill you myself."

Charli nuzzled her legs protectively.

"You might as well hug me. I'll be dead soon enough."

I did. For all her bravado, I felt her heart pounding against mine.

"I couldn't help it, Kathryn. Your showing made everything perfect. Only an idiot wouldn't try to retrieve the notebook tonight."

Bob Baker spoke at last. "A decent woman wouldn't do what you's doin'."

Charli rewarded him with a warning look and a growl.

His voice grew placating. "Please, Miss Trent. Don't publish that book. Destroy it. She don't deserve no more pain."

"She?" I asked, wondering what Connie or Jenni had done that their father had gone to such lengths to cover up.

"You have been advised to seek counsel," Cole said, Boy Scout that he was. "Anything you say now can be used against you."

"That don't matter," Bob replied, his stance determined. "You can take me to jail. Just don't publish that book."

Gertrude leafed through the notebook in her hand, pretending to find its contents very interesting. "I don't see how any of this could hurt the girls." She took a shot in the dark.

"Not them," Bob said, shaking his head. "Bessie."

"Bessie?" The word slipped out of my mouth before I could stop myself.

Bob Baker suddenly looked old. His breathing didn't seem either regular or strong. He glanced around the room and said, "Can I sit down?"

Cole directed him to the edge of the bed.

Staring at his hands in cuffs, Baker said, "She didn't mean to kill him."

"Bessie killed Guy Tortelli?" Phil asked.

Baker nodded. "He was always after her, pestering her with questions about her past, about why her husband left and about her childhood. I saw it all happen. He'd grabbed her by the elbow and she'd twisted loose. He must have said something really hurtful because she pushed him. He fell and hit his head, hard."

"What did Bessie do?" Cole asked quietly.

"She ran home, scared to death."

"So you took care of the body for her?" Gertrude urged him to continue.

"I knew you was at one of your meetings and the easiest way of getting rid of him was that old freezer. I figured maybe by the time anybody found him, Bessie'd be dead and buried and her secrets wouldn't matter anymore.

"I buried Wilson by the river," he added regretfully.

I was trying to visualize Bessie killing anyone and having an even harder time figuring out why Bob Baker went to such lengths to protect her. Gertrude must have been wondering the same thing.

"So you didn't want anyone to know about Bessie's behavior, her past?" Gertrude asked sympathetically.

"You read his notebook. How would you feel if he were writing about you?"

Gertrude shook her head meaningfully. Bluffing, she said, "Why, bad. I'd feel real bad."

"You'd be heartbroken," Bob said. "I never should have done it."

Now I was totally confused, from the look in the detectives' eyes I wasn't sure they were seeing things any clearer than I.

As though he'd held a secret inside like a tapeworm, Bob said, "I was the one that told Don Turner his wife was dangerous. I was a fool. It's just that it spooked me the way she turned her boy's life around. One minute her son was dying, like so many others, of polio. The next day, he's fit as a fiddle.

"When Don asked me what I thought, I'd never expected him to up and leave her. Take the boy away. I've tried to look after the house a bit for her over the years, but she's never seen little Danny since."

Baker gazed up at us, anguish painted on his face. "I lost my wife. If I'd a lost my girls, I don't know how I woulda survived."

As Cole and Phil led him out of the room, I couldn't help wondering how he would survive now, in jail, without the girls.

Gertrude sank heavily on the bed, the fake notebook beside her.

"So who's the bad guy?" I asked wearily.

Gertrude took my hand in hers and said, "Kathryn, there are some. Not this time. This time we just have people, trapped in their mistakes, doing the best they can."

I tipped my head onto Gertrude's shoulder. She patted my cheek with one hand and stroked Charli's head with the other.

"Poor Bessie," I said. "She really has had some bad breaks."

"Yes, she has." Gertrude got that look in her eye, the one I'd started to recognize as trouble. "She has."

"Gertrude?"

"So, Kathryn," she fenced neatly. "How was the showing?"

"The showing!" I'd forgotten all about it. "It went great. It was great. It's probably over by now."

"Well, why don't you go find out, eh? I need a lay-down. Horizontal. Get me my eye pillow, will you?"

By the time Nakita leapt to the bed and curled at the top of her head, I think she may already have been asleep.

The day of the estate sale seemed to almost arrive too soon. Because of Gertrude's grounds and the amount of goods for sale, the event held almost a carnival atmosphere.

Gertrude had obtained a high-powered attorney to represent Bob Baker. We were all hoping that due to extenuating circumstances and considering his age and health any sentence would be reduced to probation.

Connie and Jenni couldn't think of enough ways to thank Gertrude. Consequently, Maid for You not only put the house in perfect order, but staffed the sale as well.

"So, Kathryn," Gertrude said, as we took a final stroll across her lawn. "You've done quite well for yourself."

That was an understatement. Between the sales at the opening and my commission off this job, my special building fund was full and more. The lithograph was authentic—$15,000. That Warhol Postum? It was the only one of its kind, signed expressly *To Gertrude from Andy.*

"Yes, and the best part was getting to know you, Gertrude," I said, meaning it. "I'll never forget you."

"Poppycock. Thanks just the same. Look." She gestured with her cane toward the sidewalk where Bessie was walking with a middle-aged man at her elbow.

That big-shot attorney had gotten Bessie off the hook using a questionable self-defense strategy. Somehow it had worked. Apparently Bessie had never thought Guy to be dead; she simply remembered him as another man who had paid her attention and disappeared.

Meanwhile, Gertrude had used her connections to locate Danny Turner, whose father had died years before. Danny had been told that his mother was dead, and now he could hardly wait to meet the woman he recalled as being ''his angel.''

We kept walking toward them. I hailed the couple.

'' 'Morning, Kathryn,'' she said, a glow of serenity softening her worn expression.

'' 'Morning, Bessie,'' I replied.

''I believe you've met my son, Danny Turner,'' she went on with noticeable pride.

Danny, who had his mother's eyes, looked as happy as a man can who's been reunited with the mother that he'd thought he'd lost so long ago.

Bessie gestured for me to join her a few feet away. I complied.

''I want to thank you,'' she said softly.

''You already have.'' My heart felt so full of happiness for her that I couldn't imagine a greater reward.

She thrust her clawlike hands through the chain-link and grasped mine. Puzzled, I looked into her steady, fixed gaze as she drew my hands and hers over to my midsection.

Suddenly, my hands began tingling. Heat seemed to flow from her to me to my stomach. It felt like golden fingers reaching beneath my flesh, massaging my insides. I was at once peaceful and a bit frightened.

''There,'' she said, at last, releasing me. ''It's done. Forget the burdock.''

''Okay,'' I said, somewhat in a daze as she walked back to her son.

My stomach felt unusually light, deliciously empty. Had

she? Stranger things have happened, I told myself. Only time would tell.

Gertrude was alone when I rejoined her.

"Do you think she'll move now?" I asked. "Live with her son?"

Gertrude appeared thoughtful. "I don't know. I believe whatever she does, he won't be far away."

"You're a good woman, Gertrude," I told her.

"Shh. Somebody might hear you, ruin my reputation."

"I doubt if anyone could touch that," a deeply masculine voice said.

I turned to discover an Omar Sharif lookalike ducking under the low-hanging branches of a mulberry tree.

"Gertrude," he said, smiling in a way that had *my* knees weak. "It's good to see you."

"Ahmad," she replied warmly. In explanation to me she said, "Ahmad heard I was moving and he's kindly offered to have me as guest on his estate."

"There were quite a few offers once the RIO heard she was still in action," the man said.

In reply to my puzzled expression, he whispered, "Retired Intelligence Officers." So this was one of those "scary retired agents" who might have rearranged Cole's face. Not bad.

"I haven't decided yet," Gertrude said, tipping her nose higher. "But it's lovely to have choices."

Ahmad offered her his arm. With her hand tucked in the crook, she looked back over her shoulder at me and said, "I've always been mad about foreign men."

Somehow she managed to swing that bad hip of hers, just a bit.

A familiar bark caught my attention. I glanced up in time to see Charli barreling toward me. He looked so happy when he was running.

I stooped to greet him and as I rubbed my hands over his fur I realized that Gertrude and I had a lot of choices to make. I finally had enough money to move where I pleased. Perhaps with me out of the house, Dad would get the gumption to finally propose to Jewel.

I had my art career and my business, and of course there was Gary . . . and perhaps, Cole?

The possibilities lay before me glittering like diamonds in the grass.